FRITZI COX

ISBN-13: 978-1-7364167-1-6

FROM THE DESK OF FRITZI COX

IT WASN'T LONG AFTER my travels to Morningwood that I was called back on an urgent assignment. Once my article on the world's most haunted small town had broken, several residents had reached out and asked if I could tell their stories too. Some events I couldn't quite understand because I'd recently been sealed off from the magical realm and all its creatures. I could no longer prove the truth in their tales. So, stories were the only link connecting our worlds. It was all we had.

My visit with the fantastical was thrilling but brief. The unpleasant experience left me shaken, confused, annoyed, and after a while, craving more.

As the old saying goes, we never know what we have until we lose it. These days, I feel preoccupied with dreams of my old hometown and the stories within begging to be told. I've had to rely on human accounts and witnesses or my once-mythical husband to fill in the missing pieces during my research.

But that hasn't stopped me from reporting. Plenty of locals have had encounters with the supernatural. Their demanding insistence for interviews sparked my motivation to continue on this journey. They need not only validation, but also an outlet or sounding board—me.

One of these residents is a newcomer by the name of Princess Penelope. Her quick wit and bubbly persona drew me in, as if she'd cast a spell, mesmerizing my thoughts with her many charms. But that was impossible for Penelope. She couldn't charm a fly off a frog turd. The poor woman's magic had begun to die slowly, turning her into—as she put it—"a sad sack of stupid human bones." She couldn't figure out why her powers had begun disappearing or why she now straddled the line between the human and supernatural realm. To our knowledge, living in both worlds was impossible for most of us.

It didn't take much convincing for me to help. If I could figure out how to get her fully back into the magic realm, perhaps I could return at will too. But Princess Penelope had more in mind than answers. As soon as her skills had faded, so had her fiancé's love. Her Prince Not So Charming had taken her lack of magic as a hit to *his* ego.

Once his favorite enchanted mirror had become a total asshole, roasting him at every pass, he'd had enough of Penelope's sudden disgrace. Prince Jerkface had thrown the princess and the rest of her broken friends out of his kingdom forever, leaving her a woman scorned. And scorned she was. Just as charming as she could be, there lay a deadly urge for vengeance simmering below her surface. This jilted bride wanted back more than her powers.

After she settled into an abandoned cottage, shame-faced and hiding deep within the forest of Morningwood, Penelope began working tirelessly on a plan to pay her ex-lover his dues. She consulted with witches, dabbled in black magic, and even practiced a hex that would grow the victim's—aka Prince Not So Charming—nose hairs inches on the hour until they became long enough to wrap around his neck, choking him in their scratchy grip. For this reason alone, he couldn't sleep for more than two hours at a time and forever had to keep a pair of trimmers in his back pocket.

But all of her practicing barely taught Penelope anything. Her magic flickered in and out like static on my mother's old television set. Sometimes, I could see the princess and hear everything she'd said. Other times, she appeared like a wisp of smoke before vanishing for days. I desperately wanted to help find her magic again. But as my time in Morningwood had taught me, some things weren't meant to be. Sometimes, we stumbled and never got back up.

The last interview I had with Penelope was before the ball at Bostwick mansion, where the fragile princess began to mix her charm with a much more sinister audience. The last events she recollected back to me were sometimes dark enough to turn my stomach but, at other times, fascinating enough to keep me coming back for more. Once she mentioned the vampire brothers who ran the local winery, I immediately became hooked. Their mission was something that could aid in opening the supernatural world to both of us once again.

But alas, after she told me their secrets, I never heard from the princess again.

I don't know what happened to Penelope. She's disappeared from my life entirely, which means she must have solved the code and forever returned to the realm of magic, or her vampire friend sealed her fate with his alluring bite. Either way, I was devastated. I spent countless hours trudging through the forest, searching for her cottage, and I even took a few dangerous trips to Bostwick Winery to look for clues of her whereabouts. But the mansion was closed for repairs, and I saw nothing else out of the ordinary at any of these locations. Sadly, my vision only reached as far as my human eyes could take me.

When Penelope had first asked if I could write her story, she'd begged me to call out her asshole ex and squash his big ego for good. As my once-genie husband would say, her wish was my command. But the tragic princess deserved better … more. She needed her happily ever after, and despite my reservations about her new, ominous friends, I would write her one.

I can't recount every detail or fact-check every rumor. Because of my inability to do so, this is a work of fiction. Some names have been changed to protect egos, lives, and myself, except for Prince Not So Charming—aka Theodore Fuckwad. He's real.

Once upon a time, there lived a jilted bride by the name of Princess Penelope. This is her story.

ONE

PENELOPE

"Bunch of damn lunatics," I muttered, slamming the door behind me.

Raindrops pelted against my cheeks like stinging little frost fairies, but I didn't care. The woods surrounding my crumbling cottage had come to be my escape over these last few weeks. As my so-called friends had pushed me to work harder, they'd instead ended up pushing me right out of the door and into the sketchy woods surrounding my house. Rumor had it, the forest was full of smelly trolls, killer goblins, and beastly werewolves.

I didn't mind that last part so much. Werewolves ruled Morningwood, and from the glimpses I'd had of the leading pack, they could eat me up anytime. Although I'd only ever met one real werewolf, I was sure he could ravage me raw in the moonlight before transforming and letting me ride through the woods on his hairy back à la forest princess. That scenario would have shocked my old kingdom, Poppycock.

But instead of living on the edge, I'd planned to settle into the life of a harmless fairy-tale princess and marry a prince who was anything but charming. Not to mention, he couldn't ravage shit. The best he could do between the sheets was when I put Mirror Mirror in front of our bed, so he could basically fuck himself. At first, the enchanted mirror was Theodore's biggest fan. He cheered on my fiancé every night we made love.

"You're a rock star in bed!" Mirror Mirror used to say.

Or he would throw out compliments such as, "You devilish man. Look at the way your shoulders flex when you're in that position! How masculine! How beastly! How ferocious!" And then he would growl.

None of these compliments were true.

Mirror Mirror had specifically been charmed to be full of positive affirmations and motivational energy—that was, until he became a total asshole. Things quickly went downhill when I changed. Once my powers began to fade, the rest of Prince Theodore's castle became dark and dreary. When Mirror Mirror had seen Theo last, he'd likened him to a were-bear—and not because of his manly ferocity. But because my ex had hair long enough on his back and butt that I sometimes wondered if I could braid it. Maybe I'd thread tiny bows on the ends, decorating him like a Christmas tree.

"Quit lying to yourself, Penny," I said, stomping through the soggy leaves.

As much as I hated him these days, I had a hole in my heart the size of my fairy godmother's big mouth. I loved Theo. Stupidly. Crazily. Loved Theo. But that type of man could only love himself, and I had some major mental obstacles to overcome to understand why I fell for men wearing capes sewn from red flags.

But I didn't have time for that yet. My current mission was to build myself up, bring back my superpowers, and make that jerk see what he'd lost. Then, I could hopefully continue my life with sweet and loving, supportive and communicative, emotionally available and healthy men—or a beastly werewolf. I wasn't *too* picky. After all, I was a princess. I had parties to attend and events to throw and a life to live.

I trudged my way toward the clearing I'd built to practice my spells in peace. My fairy godmother, Gertie, had tried to reteach me at home, but between her constant pressure and my ruthlessly enchanted household, I couldn't focus. None of my so-called helpers actually helped me. I never got the crystal slippers the other godmothers magicked up, nor did Mirror Mirror ever compliment my sharp bone structure and glowing skin—when I'd had it.

And worst of all, Pumpkin, that stupid enchanted vegetable of Godmother's, was the perviest pumpkin I'd ever met. If I opened the shower curtain, he was there. If I rolled over in bed, he was there. I'd once threatened to carve him up and pull his guts out through his mouth, but he'd only laughed and wiggled his drawn-on brows.

The only friend I could rely on in my screwed-up cottage was my pet fox, Trevor. Clever Trevor. The poor thing smelled atrocious, but he made up for it in loyalty.

Usually, he accompanied me on my walks, but I'd patted him on the head good-bye and left him home this evening. I needed my entire focus on my signature spell. Not long ago, I could belt out a few hums and summon woodland creatures to do my bidding—that was how I'd met Trevor. But lately, when I belted out those same hums, I only summoned a cock-eyed rabbit, a gassy wind spirit, and an intellectual cockroach who liked to debate quantum physics. Never had I wanted to squash a bug as much as I did that self-proclaimed genius.

After that fiasco, I'd dismissed my *pets* and declared myself a failure, refusing to attempt the summons again until I had at least learned a simpler task, such as flicking my wrist and setting my mop to work. And that little accomplishment had happened this morning. Although my mop might have gone a little crazy and attacked my face for a split second, I'd still made it do my bidding or cleaning.

Winning.

I had a suspicion that my magic faded with age, like estrogen, draining youth and power from my body, turning me into an old crone soaked in wine, and leaving me with an excessive amount of bitter baggage. At least, that was how I felt at thirty-one, past my prime. I'd stupidly wasted my youth on a man who put off marrying me for so long, only to dump me at the altar and banish me from his life and his kingdom, all in a matter of minutes.

I groaned, settling down onto a tree stump caked with a questionable fungus. The drizzle of rain dissolved into a mist, wrapping around me in a blanket of wet gloom and matching my mood. Anger bubbled inside me like a cauldron of witch's brew, ready to explode and destroy its next victim.

Could this be early menopause? I thought with a sudden pang of panic.

"Ahem," I cleared my throat and shook the thought from my head, determined to focus on something I'd not tried yet—the darker creatures of the forest.

My spells usually involved singing birds, cuddly bunnies, and doe-eyed deer. But there was one time, a while back, I'd accidentally summoned a rabid alligator. Of course, I'd hidden up in a tree until he left, but I always wondered if my charms could be used for more than sweet, princessy qualities, as my ex used to put it. You know, those things I'd lost when I became a worthless *humanish* bag of bones.

"*Fa-la-la-la, rawr, la-la-la,*" I tried, bellowing out the lowest spooky tone I could.

But nothing happened.

"I said, *fa-la-la-la, rawr, la-la-la!*" I screamed into the clearing, but only the windswept leaves echoed back.

I scuffed my boot into the dirt, kicking a pebble across the way before taking a deep breath and trying again.

"La-la-la, rawr, la-la-la." My voice rang out as it had years ago when my magic was strong and powerful enough to command an army of squirrels, nibbling the ankles of all my enemies.

A blanket of clouds thickened overhead, forming a sinister chill in the air. The hair on the back of my neck prickled. I had a feeling I wasn't alone anymore.

"La-la-la, rawr, la-la-la," I sang again, louder.

Footsteps, much heavier than a bunny's, pattered behind me. I stood up and threw my hands in the air, still singing and ignoring the feeling of someone watching me. I twirled, singing in harmony with the wind in the trees, the drizzle of rain, and the low hum of the clouds growing overhead. My senses awakened to the natural life around me, and for the first time in a year, I felt whole again.

I spun around the clearing, singing my heart out and skipping through the mud until—as my luck would have it—a man, not a beastly creature under my command, walked into my life.

"You rang," said a deep voice behind me.

I turned to see a tall, dark figure stepping out of the shadows. His mouth curled, as if on the edge of laughter, displaying a glimpse of two deadly sharp fangs.

"Holy shit. I summoned a vampire." I stood frozen, unable to look away.

He towered over me like a great oak tree. His pale skin, from an obvious lack of sunlight, magnified the inky blackness in his eyes.

"Actually, you didn't. I was joking." He held his massive hands up and shrugged.

"Wait, so you aren't here to do my bidding?" I blushed, realizing this beautiful creature had seen me stomping around and singing like a madwoman. So much for my forest-princess pipe dream.

"That depends on what your bidding is." He loomed closer.

I could smell Bostwick Black Label, my favorite wine, on him. I shamefully knew that plum, leathery scent anywhere. I'd practically lived on bottles of it during the early stages of my breakup. Either this vampire shared my love of fine wines or he'd just eaten a heartbroken, hot mess of a maiden, such as myself.

"I want to gain back my powers, destroy my evil ex-boyfriend, and claim Poppycock as my own. Maybe throw some world domination in there afterward. That's all." My voice trembled.

His gaze sent tingles throughout my body, ricocheting off my damp skin.

"Why didn't you say so?"

He moved swiftly, stopping inches before me. I wasn't a short woman by any means, but next to this hunk of death, I couldn't even see over his shoulders. His long fingers reached out, curling beneath my chin and lifting my gaze to his. A shiver crept up my spine, but my fight-or-flight mechanism betrayed me. I couldn't move. Mr. Vamp had me caught in his vampish stare.

"Are you mesmerizing me?" My eyes darted back and forth, searching his.

"I don't know. Am I?" He stared back.

"No, you know, the thing you vamps do. Hypnotize! That's it. You're hypnotizing me. Don't think I don't know it. Just because I can't move doesn't mean I can't run my mouth."

"Obviously."

"What was that?"

"I'm not hypnotizing you. You're free to do as you please." He took a step back and bowed, extending his long and well-muscled arms to his sides.

"Damn right, I am! You're looking at Ms. Independent." I broke away and crossed my arms over my chest.

"Yes, so I heard. Ms. World Domination. But I think you might have a better career in music. Those notes you hit sounded lovely, like a birdsong."

"Really? Good. Because lately, they'd been sounding like a stray cat in heat—all scratchy and snarly and desperate. Pitiful too." I huffed, brushing my bangs out of my face.

"It sure didn't sound like a noise I'd ever heard a witch make. You ladies normally cackle and caw like crows. You're different." He ran his hands through his unruly black hair. Even his basic movements were delicate and graceful. This man was more regal and princessy than me.

"What did you call me?" I asked. My shoulders tensed at his insult.

I stared down at my muddy boots, my frayed skirt, and the buttons missing from my blouse. I looked no more like royalty than the damn smelly troll living in my shed. He'd come with my place, unfortunately, and my soft spot for ugly creatures kept me from giving him the boot.

"A witch. You said you wanted your powers back. I'm assuming you belong to a coven?" He cocked his head to the side, studying me like a monster toying with its prey.

"I'm not a witch! I'm a princess! Good grief. Do I look like I have a bulbous nose with a wart on the side? Or do I smell like eye of newt and a rancid beaver tail?"

"No. You look absolutely delicious, and you smell"— he took a deep breath before licking his fangs—"divine."

"Thanks. Witches aren't the only women with power, you know. Princesses can do stuff too."

"I'm aware. I just didn't think I would be so lucky to meet a beautiful princess on my grounds. It's dangerous out here. Too dangerous for someone like you."

"Your grounds? You live here? I didn't think Morningwood had vampires!" I craned my neck, peering into the woods around us and bracing myself to be attacked by more vamps. I wasn't entirely opposed to the idea. He wasn't a werewolf, but I'd heard the filthy things vampires were capable of—if they kept their teeth to themselves. Mostly.

"They do now. Five of us. I'm Vail," he said, sticking his hand out for me to take.

"I'm Penelope." I gave him a lifeless grip and dipped my head.

He brought the back of my hand to his mouth, brushing his lips across my knuckles. I hadn't had a man pull that move on me since I was a teenager. Men these days were all about firm handshakes and dumb head flicks. But Vail was probably from a different era, centuries ago.

The clouds parted overhead, illuminating the forest floor with the tiniest sliver of sunlight between us.

"Uh-oh." He stiffened, dropping my hand.

"You going to catch on fire?" I looked up at the sky.

"No. We wither away slowly, fading into a pile of hot ashes. We don't spontaneously combust! How disgraceful!" he said, touching his collar, as if I'd deeply offended him.

The stream of sunlight grew, beaming down into the entire clearing. Vail's beautiful, pale skin began to smoke.

"I'm afraid our plans for world domination will have to wait. Good day, Princess Penelope. Be careful who you sing to. These woods are full of things much more vicious than you." He flinched at a spark behind his ear before disappearing into the trees.

"Oh yeah? Like what?" I shouted after him.

"Like me," he called back.

"Pfft. You didn't seem so scary to me," I muttered, turning to head back home.

Meeting a vampire in *my* woods was enough drama for me to call it a day. Besides, the ominous feeling that had come with Vail still lingered in the air after he left. I wasn't so sure I wanted to stay any longer. But maybe I could convince my ex to come for a visit and meet my new toothy friends.

TWO

VAIL

I LAY ON A COT in our underground chamber while my brother Finn tinkered in the laboratory. The potion I'd tested earlier this evening was supposed to allow me to absorb sunlight for at least five minutes. Granted, we hoped to eventually develop the vaccine to last longer, but we were still in the early stages of our discoveries. Hence, me, the guinea pig in today's failed trial.

"Hold still. I need a sample of your blood and the charred skin across your forearm. Jeez. I don't think that batch worked at all. You said this happened as soon as the sunlight hit you?" Finn asked, scraping my skin with a scalpel.

"Yep. I started smoking right as the clouds parted." I flinched as he peeled a piece of skin from my arm and placed it in a petri dish.

"Damn it. The last batch lasted three minutes. This should've lasted at least five. I'll have to run more labs and see where I screwed up." Finn grabbed a syringe and pulled my arm straight before jabbing the needle into the crook of my elbow.

"Hey! I might not be human, but I can still feel pain!" I cried out, baring my fangs at my brother.

"Only of the physical kind for now. Wait until our mission is complete and the spell is broken. You'll feel every whisper of pleasure, every heartbreakingly sad song, every blissful moment, and every ounce of desperation and grief in our manufactured hearts." He pulled the needle out of my arm and pushed a cotton ball to the wound before bandaging it.

"One day," I said.

"In our lifetime." He gathered his medical tools and samples and set them on a nearby workstation, plugging away at a computer.

"That's because we live forever." I sat up, rubbing the slightly charred skin on my forearm.

"Not for long."

"You really think you're getting close to curing vampirism?" I walked to his computer, blinked at the numbers on the screen, and shook my head. I couldn't make sense of any of it.

Finn was the intellectual in our brotherhood. He could run DNA sequences—whatever the hell that was—all while decoding spells and brewing a cure for the Witch Itch. I knew. I'd had it after a nasty run-in with some witch named Karen years ago.

"I think we'll be successful at it. As long as our efforts aren't … delayed." His fingers flew across the keyboard.

"You mean, stopped," I said.

"Precisely."

"I don't think a small brotherhood of vamps running a winery in Morningwood will raise suspicion. Besides, we're hardly the only vamps who want to feel again. I've come across plenty in my years who wish they could feel breath in their lungs."

"True. But there are a lot more vamps who love being at the top of the food chain, and you know those bastards will do *anything* to keep us there."

"Has Leo mentioned anything else about it?" I asked, inspecting the plastic models of human hearts lining his desk.

"Not a word. But he has Drake out scouting every night anyway. Between you and me, if The Council hears about our little experiment, they'll stake us before we've gathered enough data to give us hope for a flush in our cheeks again."

I scrubbed a hand over my tired eyes. "Whatever lifestyle we choose is dangerous, and I'm sick of it. If we feed on humans, we're murderers. If we attempt to fix our … *cravings* … we betray our species. Either way, we alert the authorities. I'd rather live a normal life. Maybe settle down and have a family one day. But I'm guessing there's no way to make our sperm alive again either since we can't even make ourselves alive yet."

He laughed. "I'll take your blood samples. But don't ask me to take your sperm samples too."

My thoughts leaped to the wild beauty I'd met in the forest. Her petite, flowerlike stature would crumble in my deadly hands. I couldn't imagine taking her as mine if I wanted to. Someone as pure as Penelope couldn't handle a villain like me.

"I won't. Not yet. But maybe one day. If you make a heart and our blood come alive, then the rest of us might wake up too." I shrugged, stretching my arms over my head and yawning.

"You have a lot of faith in me. I'll do my part down here. You just bring me investors and work your charisma, so we can harvest more human DNA."

"On it." I waved good-bye and shuffled my feet to bed. It was well past my bedtime, but sunlight waited for no vamp. And I needed those rays to complete my mission to feel again.

I longed to have a fluttering in my chest from new love or even a pang of jealousy rip through me like a knife. But vampires didn't feel emotion like humans. Once we turned, all of our feelings left with our souls, except for the basic animalistic instincts: fight or flight, hunger, sleep, and procreation—without actual procreation.

I tiptoed down the halls until I made it to my darkened bedroom. The rest of the brothers were sleeping on schedule. The eldest, Leo, kept to a strict and militaristic routine. His drive was similar to mine in that he was an overachiever at anything he put his mind to. The only difference between us, besides a hundred years or so, was he went about things more clearheaded and cutthroat. I wouldn't be a part of the Bostwick brotherhood if it wasn't for him. All of us brothers shared the same need to return to our human selves, but Leo was the boss man who would get us there. A former lieutenant in his past life, he had the strength to carry our mission through.

I walked to the window in my room and pressed my palm to the blinds, wishing I could open them and let fresh air inside. I wanted to sniff the autumn breeze and feel the warmth of the setting sun on my skin. But I didn't have a death wish tonight. I had an alive wish. And I wanted nothing more than to be the Prince Charming I once had been.

"Rise and shine, dipshits!" my brother Ian called, banging on the doors down the hall.

I rolled over in bed, groaning at the tight pull of skin across my burned arms. After my run-in with Penelope and the sun, I'd completely forgotten we were nearing harvest.

"Coming, coming!" I shouted back after he knocked a second time. The splintered wooden door rattled on its hinges, teetering on the brink of collapsing under Ian's farmhand strength.

I pressed my heels to the floor and rose out of bed.

"Let's go! Moon's overhead, and the grapes are ready now. Any delay, and they'll be as bitter as you assholes," Ian said.

I stretched my back before quickly dressing and heading downstairs. A dull ache of hunger shot through my veins, pulling me from my sleepiness.

"Here, take this. When was the last time you fed?" Leo handed over a glass of Project X, our special wine, reserved only for vampires.

I sipped the thick liquid and winced.

"Gnome blood? Really?" I asked.

"Sorry. It's all we have until we get more donators on board. It's not entirely difficult to find those who want to end vampirism, but getting them to donate blood is another story. They think we'll become addicted and drain them. I didn't have the heart to tell the gnome he tasted like a rancid carrot." Leo patted my shoulder.

"That's it!" I snapped my fingers. "That's exactly what gnome blood tastes like. Rancid garden vegetables."

"Speaking of rancid, if y'all don't get out there and start picking those grapes, they'll be as tough as the back side of a saddle," Ian said, motioning for us to head outside.

"You heard the cowboy! Let's yeehaw into the night. Maybe hunt some wild game after. The woods have been noisy lately." Drake flew down the stairs, beating us to the door.

My shoulders tensed at the mention of the woods. If any of my brothers ever came across Penelope, I wasn't so sure they could control themselves—especially Drake since he was still learning how to control his appetite. Hell, I'd had a hard time keeping my fangs from showing after watching her twirl around the clearing. She'd moved like a maelstrom, awakening everything in her path. Her thick blonde curls whipped back behind her as she opened her rosy mouth and sang the most lovely and terrifying melody I'd ever heard. She'd claimed she was a princess, but Penelope had something more—something darker—in her blood, whether she knew it or not.

"The only thing I'm getting into after this is my bed. I've got creatures to woo, funds to find, and more trials with Finn." I rubbed my eyes and followed my brothers to the barn.

"Speaking of funds"—Leo cleared his throat—"I found someone who has contacts for the winery. I think we can trust him. We'll need more on our team to host the tastings and harvest the DNA along with this." He waved his hands at the endless rows of grapes we passed.

"More dayworkers. We need someone who knows the business and the vineyards. Randy and James are our only dayworkers. They can't keep up. With all the orders we're getting, we need more hands on deck at all times." Ian opened the barn doors and turned on a light, illuminating a pile of dusty tools and a rusted, old tractor.

I picked up a pair of sheers, turning it in my hands. The only time I spent performing manual labor was during planting and harvesting, both of which were new to me. I hadn't lived at Bostwick long.

"So, who is this contact?" Drake asked.

"He's someone I'd like to ally with. It'd be a smart move. His name's Antonio. He runs the local sheriff station … with his pack." Leo grabbed a basket out of the barn.

"A pack? You've got to be kidding me!" Drake threw his hands in the air, letting them fall to his sides in a loud smack.

"Did you not hear the part where I said they run the local sheriff station? We need them, and since they naturally hate vampires, they'll do what it takes to help find a cure and get rid of us. Besides, he seems like a decent man." Leo stomped through the dirt toward the vines.

The brothers and I grabbed our things and followed on his heels.

"But werewolves?" Drake groaned.

Leo threw his basket down and swiftly backtracked to Drake, blocking him from moving.

"Do you question my judgment?" Leo asked, snarling. A gleam of moonlight reflected off his bared fangs.

"No. Not at all. I just—" Drake took a step back.

"Good," Leo said.

"I trust you know what you're doing. If you say these werewolves are good for us, I believe you, and I'm behind you one hundred percent." Drake straightened his shoulders and craned his neck, looking up toward Leo, who stood over a foot taller than him.

"Does anyone else take issue with forming an alliance with the wolves?" Leo shouted, glancing at both Ian and me.

We shook our heads.

"It's done then. He'll be here soon to meet with us, and moving forward, we'll have more help and more workers." Leo shoved his hands into a pair of leather gloves. "Let tonight be the first night of a new era. Vampirism is dead."

"Literally," I muttered, rolling up my sleeves before beginning to work.

The howling of wolves echoed through the forest.

THREE

PENELOPE

"IT'S TOO EARLY TO rise," I groaned, throwing my arm across my eyes and blocking out the sunlight filtering through my drafty bedroom window.

Trevor stirred at my feet, lazily flicking his bushy tail back and forth, swirling whirls of dust in the morning light.

"Nonsense. You're to start on your spells immediately. Look at this place! It's a disaster. If you can't make your forest friends clean it or your enchanted supply closet, you'll need to do the work yourself." Gertie clicked her tongue.

"Up and at it, bitch. Even though you need all the beauty sleep you can get with those deep wrinkles running along your forehead. If I had ivy seeds, I'd plant them in those trenches and let the vines cover up that ugly face of yours," Mirror Mirror said.

"One more rude comment out of you, and I'll shatter you into a million pieces and scatter your shards across Troll City. The only thing you'll be reflecting is what you see up the skirts of hairy trolls," I snapped, jumping out of bed.

The pervy pumpkin lying next to me bounced, rolling over onto my pillow and grinning so wide that a few seeds sputtered out of his makeshift mouth.

"And you"—I pointed at him—"get your own room, or I'll carve you into the stupidest jack-o'-lantern you've ever seen. I'll give you buck teeth and googly eyes. Maybe stick a limp pickle in you for a nose."

"Good heavens! What kind of princess speaks like that? You were never this … brazen and grumpy at the castle." Gertie shook her head, plucking the empty wine bottles from my nightstand and shoving them into a trash bag.

"Back at the castle, everyone worked right. Mirror Mirror wasn't an asshole, this pumpkin wasn't even alive, and I never had to worry about cooking or cleaning. I could enjoy life, host parties, entertain, dance around my ballrooms, and travel by royal carriage. I drank champagne for breakfast and ate cake daily. Here, I'm just an old maid with a house full of misfits." I threw my hands in the air before wrapping myself in an oversize robe.

"You still drink alcohol for breakfast and eat cake like a fat kid on his birthday." Mirror Mirror's voice fell flat.

"Ahem," Gertie cleared her throat. "We'll always be this miserable unless we do something about it. That starts with a clear mind and a conscious effort to get Penelope back on her way to the throne. We'll all benefit from it. Discouragement and rude behavior won't do us any favors."

"I don't want to be Theo's princess anymore, Godmother. I want to take his kingdom and reign as an independent queen, showing him what he lost—me." I flicked my wrists to my sides and twirled, trying to transform my ragged robe into a ballgown. But I only managed a puff of smoke and a rip down the back of my pants.

"Oh dear. We have work to do." Gertie pulled a wand from her front pocket and swished it in the air, transforming my robe into a matching sweatshirt and sweatpants. My hair whipped around my face, lashing against my brow and piling atop my head into a messy bun.

"Gee, thanks. Now, I look like an old crone too. I'm sure Theo would be sorry he let this go." I shoved my hands into the pockets of my baggy pants and pulled the fabric six inches from my waist. I had gained a few pounds since I'd left the kingdom, but if my so-called friends thought I needed this size, Godmother was right. I did have work to do.

"It's work clothes. Besides, who're you trying to impress? Pumpkin?" She laughed, picking up the orange butterball. He wiggled his squiggly eyebrows.

I glanced at my reflection in Mirror Mirror, who stuck his tongue out and blew a raspberry.

"I'm not into veggie kink. But I did meet someone," I said.

The mere mention of my brief meeting with Vail sent a flush through my cheeks. Royal families didn't rub elbows with beastly creatures. But then again, I wasn't royalty anymore.

"Who? And where? In town?" Gertie set Pumpkin on the floor. He rolled to the edge of the bedroom and perched atop a pile of dusty, old spell books.

"In the woods," I answered.

A forceful gale blew across the window, rattling the thin glass pane in its frame.

"Ominous," Mirror Mirror muttered. "I always pegged you for a centaur porker. The way you got on all fours for Theo and all. You were more like a cow than a horse though. I think you even mooed once or twice."

I grabbed a blanket off of my bed and threw it over Mirror Mirror.

"I can't see, but I can still talk. Never the brightest wand in the box, were you?" Mirror Mirror asked.

"Enough. Let her speak." Gertie flicked her wand, wrapping the blanket so tight around Mirror Mirror that if he were able to die, he'd have been strangled to death by faded, old bed linens.

"His name's Vail, and he's a vampire," I said, straightening my spine from my typical slouch.

Trevor growled, jumping to the floor and circling my feet. Mirror Mirror made muffled sounds from beneath the blanket, and Pumpkin rolled under my bed.

"A vampire!" Gertie stumbled back into the wall. "You can't mingle with those creatures! Or any creatures unless it's of the friendly woodland variety! Penelope Grace! What're you thinking?"

"I thought he seemed friendly. He was a gentleman—and our neighbor. He said this was his woods. Who does this property belong to? I thought you said a friend owned this land and that we could stay here however long we needed?"

"We can. This is Priscilla's property," Gertie said.

"Priscilla? Your witch friend who lives in Morningwood Manor? That's on the other side of town! What does she have all this for?" I motioned around my crumbling cottage, which, I had to admit, was my spirit animal these days—the rot inside my home reflecting the decay inside my soul.

As much as I tried to be, I wasn't a bubbly princess anymore. The blow to my ego from Prince Dickwad had knocked me off my unicorn. Literally. That traitorous pet had washed his hooves of me too.

"She owns Bostwick Winery, up the hills. This used to be the keeper's cottage. But they've expanded up there, and they no longer need it. Enough about my friends. Tell me about yours. This could mean trouble for us, you know. Does he know we live here?" Gertie stuck her wand out and tapped it in the air. The windows and doors locked with a click.

"I couldn't talk to him long. The sun came out, and he ran. But he was very nice. I don't think he'll give us any problems. I wonder if he lives at Bostwick though. He mentioned there were other vampires. Five of them, including him."

"Goodness gracious. This is a travesty. We need to leave these woods. It's not safe. Not with vampires," Godmother said, shifting her eyes toward the door.

"But what about werewolves? You knew they were here. And the trolls. And the rabid gnomes. And all the other crap roaming around Morningwood. You never seemed to care how dangerous they were!"

"They're all dangerous too. But nothing compares to the vamps. Wolves can be tamed. They're warm-blooded. Vampires? They're already dead. The only way to get rid of them is through sunlight."

"And a stake through the heart, too, right?" I asked.

"Through the chest. They have no heart. The stake has to pierce where the heart used to be. I know. I've seen a vampire stake himself before. For all their powerfulness, they sure do seem like miserable things. But I wouldn't count on getting close enough to stake their heart. They'd drain you before you could scream for help." She shoved her wand back into her pocket and rubbed her palms down her face.

Godmother had been an old lady since I'd known her. But in the last two minutes, she looked as if she'd aged ten more years.

I pulled my hair, tightening the bun atop my head. "Then, I guess I have work to do. Clean the house, practice spells, become powerful again, and don't get drained."

"One step at a time. But practicing spells still won't help with Vail or any vamps. Your magic—and mine—is no match for them." Gertie walked to the window, peeking out over the dew-covered bushes lining our cottage.

The rest of our yard was nothing but dead leaves and moss scattered over the forest floor. Sunlight barely trickled enough through the thick canopy of trees to grow anything.

I'd tried to plant a magic bean when we first arrived, thinking it would grow into a stalk to reach the Land of

Giants. I hoped to ask a favor of them. But instead, it grew into a snapdragon. We couldn't walk past it without it trying to bite our heads clean off. Finally, Gertie had enough; she chopped it down, fried it up, and ate it in a greasy burrito. I'd promised her that was my last attempt at gardening.

"Whose magic is a match for them then?" I asked.

"Priscilla's," Godmother breathed out her name like she was uttering a curse.

The skin on the back of my neck prickled, much like it had when Vail watched me from the shadows. I never met a witch before, like I'd never met a vampire before. I had been perfectly happy, living in my castle with sweet, innocent friends. But with my house full of misfits and my new vampire neighbor, what did I have to lose?

"I want to visit her. Maybe she can help me with the spells and let us know about the vamps." I bit my lip.

Godmother had told me about Priscilla once when I was a child. She hadn't *told* me so much as she'd *warned* me about her old friend. I knew there was very little chance of her agreeing to introduce me to the witch who drank virgin's blood to retain her youth and beauty. Then again, I was hardly a virgin.

"Grab your cloak," she answered, gathering her robe in her fists and marching to the door.

"Wait, what? Don't you want to clean first?" My pulse quickened.

Trevor curled around my feet and let out a screaming bark. I reached down, patting his head to soothe him—and me.

"To hell with this shithole. We have work to do. I don't want to end up as some vampire's late-night smoothie. My blood probably tastes like fried-apple pastries, and yours probably tastes like wine. We're doomed."

The blanket fell off Mirror Mirror, landing in a wrinkled heap on the floor.

"And despair. I'm sure the vampires would love to suck on that," Mirror Mirror said.

I stepped in front of him and narrowed my eyes, sticking my middle finger in the air and snarling at my reflection.

"Hurry now, Princess," Gertie called. "You're losing your class along with your magic!"

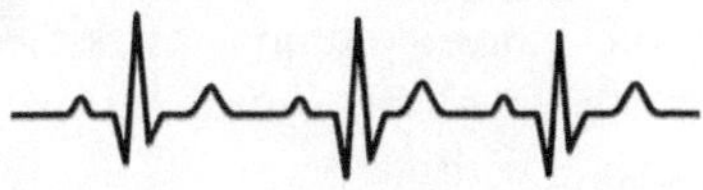

I'd only known Morningwood Manor through fabled tales from my childhood. The mansion was passed down generation after generation to an old bloodline of witches. The home was rumored to be haunted, full of traps, and cursed. Plenty of people had entered but never seemed to find their way out.

I'd heard, at the top of the manor was one long hallway, lined with doors on each side. Some doors led to sudden death or lifelong curses. But other doors led to darkness and an endless void. That was the worst way to go because if you stepped in that void, you wouldn't die. You'd only exist. You couldn't go up, and you couldn't go down. You would be alone with your thoughts. Forever.

Although the idea of being stuck in my hot mess of a mind was terrifying, the elder room struck fear in me like no other. One foot inside that door, and you were a granny for life. In this unsightly room, the victim would shrivel like a prune, shoulders slumped into a downward stoop. Their teeth and hair would fall out, and they'd always complain about aches, pains, and kids these days. It was much like a neglected nursing home in there. A victim of the elder room would age over a week or two until they turned to dust. A fine layer of victims dirtied the floor with dustballs and dander.

I'd heard plenty of rumors of other curses lurking in the mansion, but I didn't care to learn the truth now or ever. I had no plans on touring the manor, today especially. I only wanted to meet Priscilla and pick her brain on how to regain my magic. If she were as powerful as Godmother had made her out to be, this witch would be all I needed to show Theo what he was missing.

We drove up a winding hill until we reached an iron fence, complete with gigantic gargoyle statues perched on either side of the stone columns, marking the manor's driveway. The rusted iron gates squeaked open, allowing our car to putter through without pause.

I pulled the car along the paved drive in a series of jerks and stops. I hated driving. Back in the kingdom, I'd regularly traveled in style. My carriage was trimmed with gold, and I'd had only the finest white horses pulling it. But now, I had been forced to take the rusted, old car at the cottage, which had surprisingly started up easily.

The only problem was, I was a terrible driver. The first time I had driven the car with Godmother, I'd ended up in a ditch. The second time, I crashed straight into a tree. And the last time I tried, it ran out of gas. I didn't even know what gas was or why I needed it. Luckily, Antonio, the sheriff werewolf, had been friendly enough to stop and help me learn a thing or two.

I wasn't used to the modern-day society that was Morningwood. I missed the slow-paced, archaic lifestyle back in Poppycock, where we'd lived, oblivious to all these gadgets and machines. I preferred chariots to motorcycles and carrier doves to text messages—I still refused to carry a phone. If someone wanted to send me a message, they'd write a letter or send a bird.

"Can you stop slamming your foot on that fat pedal there? I'm getting nauseated, just sitting here!" Gertie pressed her fingertips to her temples and let out a muffled groan.

"Antonio said it's called the brake. And I didn't mean to! I'm doing my best." I clutched the steering wheel, swerving around a squirrel and sending my godmother slamming into the dashboard.

"Penelope!" she cried, sticking her hand out to stop herself from crashing into the windshield.

"That's why you need to strap in with this rope thing— er, seat belt!"

"I'll not be tied down to anything! What if you hurtled this thing into the river? I'd drown, trying to untangle myself!"

"Suit yourself." I stepped on the gas pedal, sending Gertie flying back into her seat as I hauled ass up the driveway, slowing only when the mansion came into view.

I swallowed hard, pushing back the growing sensation of dread in my chest.

Its cobblestone walls were cloaked in a tangle of ivy, moss, and soot, as if it was trying to camouflage itself into the surrounding woods. But it was no use. The house sat at the very top of the hill, looming over the town below. I'd always heard this hill had eyes, and now, I understood. From my vantage point, I could see everything in Morningwood.

A knot formed in the pit of my stomach as I stopped in front of the steps leading to the massive double-doored entry. Priscilla wasn't a good witch. I knew enough about her to gather that myself. Her profession, Gertie had told me, was bitchcraft—a form of spells and curses teetering on the edge of evil and often used for vengeance. If anyone knew how to disgrace an ex, it was Priscilla, the widow to many, many poor souls.

"I've never seen anything like this," I whispered. "Doubt I'd find any singing mice or dancing dusters here." My gaze trailed up the pillared columns and toward the second floor, where a row of windows was nestled into the flaking clapboard.

I rubbed the back of my neck, swatting away the sensation of something crawling along my hairline.

"Priscilla doesn't need singing mice and broomsticks. She doesn't need anything really, except youth. It keeps her alive and beautiful." Godmother slammed the door and began to walk toward the stairs.

I quickly followed in her footsteps, smoothing down my baggy sweatpants to look presentable to whatever was on the other side of the door.

"I'll need to get that recipe then," I said, brushing off the tingles on my neck again. "I've got more grays in my hair now than I did at—"

"Hello. Here to see the witch, are ye?" a rusty door knocker with a copper mustache asked in a snooty British accent.

"Is that you, Harold?" Godmother reached out, brushing her fingertips along the door knocker's brow.

He wrinkled his nose in response. "Aye, it is. My eyesight isn't as good these days, but I know a beauty when I see one. No one could ever measure up to you, Gertie. Where ye been, and what brings you back to Morningwood?" Harold asked.

"This one here." She tilted her head toward me. "We require some assistance from Priscilla. It seems my princess is losing her magic touch."

"Princess? Blimey! If I could bow, I would, but seeing as I don't have legs, the best I can manage is a wink." Harold winked his left eye, then his right, and then both.

"Pleased to meet you." I curtsied.

"The pleasure is mine. I don't get much company these days. Nothing but those vamps anyway." He rolled his metal eyes in a clink.

"The vamps. Yes. We were wondering about that. Do you know if—" Gertie started.

The door flung open, smashing Harold into the wall.

"Gertie! Dahling! Come in. Come in. And your little dog too," a petite woman as thin as a broomstick said, ushering us inside. Her curled hair was a cobweb of silvery gold, shining like a lit candle in the dark foyer. Her skin, pulled taut across her oval face, was as smooth and pale as the marble statues that lined my great halls back home. "Dreadfully sorry about Harold. He talks and talks and talks. Just like a man, he doesn't know when to zip it!"

"Priscilla, this is Princess Penelope. I'm so sorry to intrude like this. I …" Godmother fiddled with a loose thread on her skirt.

"Princess Penelope." Priscilla grinned, displaying a row of perfectly straight teeth.

The blushing pink color of her lips matched my favorite plucked roses from the gardens in my old kingdom. As nervous as I was, I couldn't tear my eyes away from the witch's beauty. I wondered which maiden had blessed her with that smile and if Priscilla had chosen her victim because of it.

"It's a pleasure to meet you, Priscilla. I've heard so much about you." I bowed my head, noticing her black velvet slippers, each one topped with a crystal broach in the shape of a spider.

"I bet you have. You'll have to tell me every last bit of gossip. But first, tea!" Priscilla turned on her heels, fanning her fur-trimmed robe out to her sides and stomping away. "Come along now. I'm sure we have a lot to discuss," she called back to us.

Gertie and I scampered after her, our obnoxiously loud footsteps echoing down the stone corridor.

"Do you live in this mansion all by yourself?" I asked, peering around each corner I passed. Once or twice, from the corner of my eye, I caught a glimpse of something or someone. But whatever apparition haunted these halls didn't want to be bothered today.

Priscilla stopped dead in her tracks, swiveling around to face me.

"My ex-husbands still hang around," she said. Her gaze shifted from me to the spiderwebs in the corners before she turned back around and marched away.

Gertie cut her eyes to mine and pressed her lips into a thin line, shaking her head in warning.

I shrugged, glancing behind me.

Priscilla led us through an arched doorway and into a gathering room decorated with wall-to-wall stained glass windows, arranged in a chaotic mosaic pattern with no rhyme or reason—unlike the stained glass hanging in my great room back home. Theo had commissioned the artist to install it after he proposed. The red and blue shards of glass framed a golden crest—the crest he'd created for himself, complete with a typical lion and sword.

"Sit," Priscilla commanded, pointing at a worn leather couch. "Stefan will bring the tea momentarily. You"—she raised her eyebrows at Gertie—"tell me everything. I know you're here for a reason. It's not like you to drop by to visit. When my gargoyles alerted me you were at the gates, I knew it must be serious."

I shuffled my feet to the couch, settling in beside Godmother on the cold leather. Priscilla sat across from us in an oversize armchair in front of the fireplace. Flames shot out from behind the chair, framing her in a flickering, sinister light, blocking any warmth from reaching us. I'd seen black eyes like hers once before when Theo made a deal with a demon. He'd told me eyes were the windows to the soul, and demons had black eyes because they had no souls. Knowing what I knew about Priscilla, I wondered if she had a drop of demon in her witch's blood.

A loud clanking came from the corridor, followed by what sounded like something dragging across the floor. Gertie reached into her pocket, grasping her wand.

"Touchy, touchy. It's just Stefan. He's my butler—and ex-husband. My fifth actually," Priscilla said.

A sickeningly green figure emerged from the doorway, dragging his feet across the floor while holding a tray of tea and cookies between his stitched hands. He grunted with each step forward.

"Is that a—is Stefan a zombie?" I pushed myself back into my seat, cringing at the sight of his gnarled arms as he set the tray of treats in front of us.

He looked like rats had chewed him.

"Why, yes, he is. They're new to Morningwood, thanks to me. My little project. This one was my favorite ex-husband. He used to buy me flowers every Friday and sing to me in the morning, and he did this thing with his tongue that made my toes curl. Naturally, I cut out his tongue and enchanted it. It still sits on my nightstand, and he … he does my bidding around here."

He bowed his head, growling, a bubbly sound escaping the slit across his throat. She patted the top of his greasy hair and sent him away.

"He doesn't talk. None of them do. I don't like a lot of small talk. So, let's begin." Priscilla poured the tea and pushed a plate of cookies across the table.

I peered into my teacup to make sure Stefan hadn't lost a finger in it and took a cautious sip. Priscilla could poison me at the drop of a witch's hat. But I had a feeling it wasn't women she had issues with.

I took in my surroundings as Godmother explained my situation. She spit out my story, no doubt rushing to silence herself, lest she talk too much too. I lost myself in the crackling of the fire, the warmth of the tea, and the scent of old parchment wafting from the bookshelves tucked neatly behind me. If this place wasn't a death trap, I'd consider it almost charming—*almost*.

"So, a man got to you too. Pity. I have a *one strike and they're out* rule. No second chances. So far, they've all struck out." Priscilla nodded toward the row of marbled male busts lining the nearby shelves.

"I don't want to kill Theo. I just want to make him sorry he ever let me go. But I can't do that when I'm … whatever I am right now. I've lost most of my power. I've even begun fading in and out of our world. Sometimes, our dimension disappears completely, and I'm lost for a confusing moment. I like being a princess. I don't want to change and be a boring, dumb human. I want to stay here and dazzle my ex into regret." I blew a breath out of my nose.

A fat, hairy spider scurried across the table, crawling up the teapot and perching itself on top. Its beady eyes rolled around the room before focusing on both Gertie and me.

"Speaking of exes, here's one now." Priscilla sighed.

"The spider?" Gertie asked, leaning forward to better look at the bug, who tapped his spindly legs in response.

"I'm no stranger to revenge. All of my ex-husbands are either dead or charmed into something. Mostly spiders. They're small, and they usually stay out of my way. They're great listeners, eavesdropping around these halls when curious guests come roaming in." Priscilla circled her fingertip along the rim of her teacup. "Stefan is the only zombie. Kenneth is a rat bastard. Really, I turned him into a rat. He should be here, but he's on assignment at the winery. It sounds to me like Theo needs to turn into something too. So, you need a charm? Cockroach perhaps?"

"No. That's all right. I just want my powers. I can take care of Theo myself." I set my tea on the table, careful not to squash her ex.

"Priscilla, pardon the change of subject. But you mentioned the winery. I know you own that and the forest surrounding it. Penelope said she met a vampire the other day by the name of Vail. He claimed we were in his woods. I'm assuming this vampire is another project of yours?" Gertie stuck out her finger and gently stroked the back of the spider. He collapsed and rolled over onto his back, exposing his belly.

Priscilla's nostrils flared. The curtains drew across the windows, the door slammed shut, and the fire faded to a dim glimmer.

"You cannot speak of that to anyone." Priscilla's voice came out low, almost growling. She rose to her feet and paced in front of us, clicking her heels on the stone. "I could kill you for knowing about that project, you know," she hissed, throwing her shoulders back and posing like a snake ready to strike.

"I didn't. We didn't. I'm so sorry. We won't mention it again," I stammered, scooting closer to Gertie. "My godmother is just worried for our safety."

Priscilla sighed. "It's not your fault. If it were, you'd be dead by now. But I know an opportunity when I see one." She cut her eyes to the doorway, locking the door with her glance. She waved her hands in the air and chanted something under her breath. A faint haze clouded the room, muffling her voice and sending a damp chill through the air. "No one can hear us now."

"I don't mean to pry, *friend*." Gertie shrugged, turning her palms up. "I mean no harm. You failed to warn me we were living next to soulless killers."

"Heartless," Priscilla muttered. "They have souls. They don't have hearts."

"Same thing. They're dead and dangerous." Godmother shook her head and helped the spider ex off the kettle before pouring another cup of tea.

"I won't lie to you. They're vicious creatures. But this particular brotherhood works for me. They're the Bostwick brothers, and I trust them—even if they are … men." Priscilla sighed, plopping herself back into her chair.

"Why do you need vampires to run the winery?" Gertie asked.

"They don't just run the winery. They're running a lab underground to … cure vampirism. They came to me with the idea late last year because they knew I needed humans— maidens. They also need humans. But the difference between them and me is, as you know, they were once human. So, they can roam the human world, whereas I, thanks to my full-blooded witch lineage, cannot."

"Why would they want to cure vampirism? Won't they die? Or be snuffed out?" I sat up in my seat.

"It's a risk they want to take. Not all vampires are happy with being vampires. Some miss their old lives, and some don't enjoy taking lives. They're not much different from us, save for their lack of a heart. Which they're studying how to build."

"A heart?" Gertie clutched her chest.

Priscilla nodded, brushing a strand of hair from her face.

"So, what do you get out of it?" I asked.

The witch turned toward me and shot me a grin through her perfectly pink lips.

"I let the vampires collect DNA at the winery to further their research in exchange for virgin maidens. Since vampires can mingle with humans, they bring me the poor girls. It's Drake who does my dirty work. Don't let his playboy charm fool you." She raised her brows. "I need maiden blood to keep me going. Otherwise, I'd be twice the age of your godmother and as powerless as you. When Drake can't bring me a lady, the vamps supply my blood. Vampire blood doesn't age, though it doesn't do anything for my beauty either. It just makes me live longer. Besides, I have enough evil in my veins. I much prefer maidens."

"I thought if you drank vampire blood, you turned into a vampire!" I gasped.

"Rumors, rumors. You have to be bitten and injected with the poison in their fangs to turn into a vamp. Not all vampires want to poison their prey. Most only want to eat. Vampire blood won't kill you or turn you. Though I've never let them bite me. It's too risky. If they get carried away, they could easily drain their victim. Not to say I haven't thought about it. If the brothers didn't work for me, I'd be covered in their bite marks. They're a devilishly delicious bunch." Priscilla traced her fingertip along her collar.

"So, let me get this straight. They bring you humans, and in exchange, you let them use an underground lab at the winery to work on curing vampirism? That explains the humming we hear coming from that side of the woods," Gertie said, scratching the side of her head. "They must be running a lot of machinery down there."

"It's a win-win situation. They're working on quite a few things over there. One in which lays this opportunity I mentioned."

"What opportunity?" I asked.

"For you to be their lab rat."

"You're going to turn me into a rat?" I cried, covering my face with my hands.

Priscilla rolled her eyes. "No … I'm going to send you to them, seeing as though you mentioned fading out of our world and into the humans'. They could learn a lot from studying you, I'm sure. Maybe bridge the dimensions even."

"What's in it for me?"

"Your godmother said the man who left you at the altar was your Prince Charming, correct?" Priscilla tapped her chin.

"Yes." My heartbeat thumped in my ears, drowning out whatever intuition I had left.

"I know the perfect man to help you show your ex what he's missing. You've already met him too."

"Who? Vail? You want me to take lessons from a vampire?" I asked.

"He's not just any vampire, Penelope. Vail was a Prince Charming long ago, too, before he was bitten. He knows better than anyone how to play the royal court game."

"Now, wait a minute." Gertie shifted her body toward me. "Penelope, are you sure you want to go through with this? Theo isn't worth putting your life in danger."

My mind bounced back to the way he'd left me at the altar, red-faced and feeling every bit as tiny as Priscilla's buggy ex-husband. Our wedding guests had avoided my eyes as I made the long walk down the aisle and out the door, crying and alone. I thought about the note he'd left on top of my suitcase, which he'd packed and had waiting in the carriage. It was cold, ruthless, and cut me like a knife. I wished I could say I hadn't seen it coming.

I tipped my chin up, meeting Priscilla's gaze.

"I'm in," I answered.

"It's settled then. Head to the winery tonight. They'll be expecting you. Remember, I like silence. Speak of this to no one. And take one of my gatekeepers with you—the gargoyle, Otto. You'll need him for communications. I've put a spell on him, so he won't turn to stone. He'll be with you always and reporting back to me."

Gertie cleared her throat. "Is he one of your ex-husbands too?"

"You know, I'm not sure. At this point, I've lost count." Priscilla cackled, twirling her billowed robe in front of her face and disappearing in a cloud of purple smoke.

Whoa, I mouthed.

"She's always had a flair for the dramatic. Come on. Let's let ourselves out." Gertie groaned, pushing herself off the sunken-in couch.

"Godmother, if we bridge the gap between dimensions, what will happen to us? Or the humans?" I swallowed hard, rising to my feet.

"I'm not sure, Princess. But let's focus on one thing at a time. You and your stubborn ass need to prove a point to Prince Asswad—Theo, not this new Prince Vamp-man. We've got a lot of work to do before I send you into battle at Bostwick. Let's go," Gertie said, rolling up her sleeves and heading toward the exit.

FOUR

VAIL

"And that concludes this evening's tasting, ladies and gentlemen. It was a pleasure to serve you in our cellar. Ian will gladly dispose of your spit cups. No need to do anything, except stop by the gift shop on the way out and pick up your favorite bottle or four," I said, dismissing our guests. My fangs strained against the caps on my teeth.

Ian began to clear the bar as humans filed out one by one, leaving their precious DNA samples behind in a warm mixture of saliva and alcohol. Those spit cups were worth more to our cause than any wine sales, but running both a lab and a winery wasn't cheap. Our funds were quickly dwindling.

"Excuse me, sir? Can you tell my wife and me a bit more about the Black Label variety? She loves a good, dark, and rustic type. And I love to *watch* her happy. Whatever she wants. Happy wife, happy life. Am I right? Do you have a wife?" an older gentleman asked Ian, pushing his unused spit cup across the countertop. He raised his thick salt-and-pepper-colored brows before shifting his gaze back and forth between his wife and Ian.

"No, sir. I've not been lucky enough to find the one for me," Ian said, tossing the cup in the trash.

The man's wife swiveled on her barstool and brushed her hair back, revealing peaked nipples under a silken blouse.

"I'd love to learn more about your wines, but it's so chilly in here. Can we go somewhere more private to talk? Do you offer tours? Can we book you?" She leaned forward, running her fingertip along her neckline. A tipsy grin played across her lips before she brought her hand to her mouth and stifled a hiccup, giggling.

"Sorry for the temperature, ma'am. It has to stay a constant fifty-five degrees for the wine. But—" Ian started.

"Ian, can I borrow you for a second?" I raised my voice, motioning for him to come to the corner where I stood, stacking glasses in the dishwasher.

He bowed his head at the couple and swiftly made his way to me.

"Their cups are empty." I pressed my lips into a thin line.

Ian raked his hand through his hair, glancing back toward the couple. "I know. I know."

"Time to be a young buck and take one for the team. Get the DNA another way." I wiped my hands on a dishrag and slung it over my shoulder.

It wasn't the first time he'd been propositioned for a threesome. Ian's quiet demeanor, coupled with his tough exterior, made him mysterious and alluring to both men and women.

"Damn. I hate my job." Ian smirked before tipping his cowboy hat and heading back to the couple.

"Right this way. It turns out, I can give a private tour tonight—off the clock." Ian flashed a boyish grin before taking the wife's hand and pulling her off the barstool.

She swayed slightly, steadying herself against the bar. "All that wine has me a bit flustered," she said.

"Shoulda spit." Ian put his arm around the lady's waist, holding her up.

Her husband stayed back, rubbing his squared jaw between his index finger and thumb while watching their interaction.

"I only swallow," she said, twirling a long blonde lock of hair around her finger.

Ian glanced back at the husband, who only nodded.

"Lucky bastard," I muttered under my breath, watching them leave.

I pulled a roll of labels out from under the bar and stuck them on each spit cup. One name per cup. I usually could remember whose was whose. It was one of the many perks of vampirism. My memory never failed. But when guests decided to swallow our wine samples instead of properly spitting them into our test kits, it screwed things up. No matter how many times I warned everyone of our high alcohol content, there was always a handful of tasters who decided being drunk was better than wasting wine.

"Ahem," came a low voice from the stairs.

I turned to catch a pair of dead eyes staring back at me.

"Leo. Hey. What's up? Everything okay?" I asked.

"Seems you have a visitor. She's here on Priscilla's account, but she said she knows you." He stood with his feet apart, hands behind his back in his formal, old war-general stance.

"I'm not sure who you're talking about." I set the labels on the counter and walked from behind the bar, pausing at an unfamiliar feeling tingling under the surface of my skin.

"It's me again! Hi. How are you?" Penelope peeked out from behind Leo, cupping her palm in a princess wave.

Her cheeks flushed pink as the caps covering my fangs popped out and rolled onto the floor, landing in front of her crystal slippers.

"Penelope! What're you doing here?" I said, scampering to pick up the caps before stuffing them in my pocket.

"I'm so sorry! I didn't mean to interrupt your DNA harvesting." She wrung her hands and took a step back, stumbling into Leo.

He cleared his throat. "Come again?" Leo tipped his head, studying the woman before him.

His posture remained unchanged, but I could see the calculations running through his mind.

"Oh! Am I not supposed to know about that? Priscilla told me everything! Well, not everything. But she sent me here to be a lab rat, so I'm assuming I'll know more soon enough. Ya know, since I'm about to give you royal blood—er, DNA. Or whatever it is I'm doing here. What am I doing here, by the way?" She looked from me to Leo and back again.

"Hey! We've got a problem!" Drake yelled, rushing down the stairs. His tousled black hair hung in his eyes.

Leo had asked Drake countless times to cut his hair and be more professional. But Drake refused, citing women called it his crowning feature. And since wooing women was his main job, he kept his tousled locks. Leo couldn't argue with that. Drake could charm the pants off of a goblin. I knew. I'd seen it.

"Not now," Leo commanded.

"Oh. Hello." Drake turned from Leo and bowed to Penelope, flashing her a toothy grin. His fangs hung low in his mouth, a signal that he was ready to fuck, fight, or eat.

I curled my fist around the tooth caps in my pocket.

"And you are?" Penelope held out her hand.

He took it, turning it in his palm, and brushed his lips across her knuckles while keeping his eyes locked on hers. Even from the other side of the room, I could see her reflection in his dilated pupils.

I pushed my tongue against my throbbing fangs, but Leo shook his head in my direction, stopping me from interfering.

"Drake Bostwick. I'm their younger brother. And you must be Princess Penelope. Priscilla told me all about you. I must say, she didn't mention how strikingly gorgeous you were. I doubt you'll be a problem at all." Drake jerked his head to the side, flicking his hair out of his eyes.

"She said I was a problem?" Penelope huffed, sticking out her chest. Her breasts rose and fell in sync with the only heartbeat I could detect in the room—hers.

Drake's fangs peeked out from under his lip.

"Drake, come with me." Leo stepped between Penelope and my brother. "Vail, handle it." He shot a look at me before pushing Drake up the stairs and out of sight.

"The nerve of that witch! I'm not a problem. How could I be? I'm a princess. I solve problems, not cause them! Did you know I once cured a season of hunger in my kingdom by twirling around a dance floor until it rained bread and butter? It lasted an entire month! This wasn't just any bread and butter either. It didn't mold. I had to hire extra help to clean it up and distribute it. Then, I slept for three weeks." She blew a breath out of her nose and walked toward me, leaning on the bar.

"Bread and butter?" I asked. "How come you didn't shoot for cupcakes or chocolates? You seem too sweet for something so … plain."

"Truth is, I tried for wine and cheese. But that was when my magic began to change, and then my Prince Not So Charming left me at the altar. So, here I am. You're to help me, and I'm to help you." She stuck her arm out and rolled up her sleeve, showing me her wrist. "Take my DNA. I'm all yours."

My fangs lowered faster than I could hide them. I tried to cover my mouth with my palm, but I wasn't quick enough. It had been days since I'd choked down a bottle of Project X.

Penelope gasped, ducking behind the bar.

"Sorry! Sorry! You're safe. It's a natural reaction. You can come out now." I threw my hands in the air, knocking over a spit cup. "Shit!" I fumbled with the sample, knocking down another.

She rose from under the bar, cringing at the sight of the bubbly liquid flowing out onto the countertop. "Ew. That's disgusting! I'd help, but I might get sick. I don't do icky stuff."

"It's all right. I got it." I grabbed a paper towel and cleaned up the mess as my fangs retracted quickly.

"I didn't mean to startle you or make you hungry. Whatever it was I did. Maybe I shouldn't have shown you my pulse."

"You didn't do anything. I'm just a vampire. We eat, we fuck, and we fight—or take flight, depending on the situation. It's our natural instincts and all we have. What we can't do is feel." I paused, throwing the towel in the trash. "That's why Priscilla sent you here, I suppose. But I'm confused as to how I'm supposed to help you. I'm afraid I can only offer you wine."

"Oh, I'll take that. But wait! There's more." She held a finger in the air. "Priscilla said you were a prince once. I need a prince to show me how to make me more princessy since my magic's fading. So I can show my ex what he gave up. Remember, world domination and all?" She ran her hands down her hourglass figure, stuck out a hip, and smirked.

"I didn't think you were serious."

"I am. I need therapy," she sighed, scraping her shoe against the cobblestone floor and avoiding my gaze.

"You know, it would be easier if you forgot about that piece of shit and moved on with your life now instead of humiliating him and destroying his ego."

"Where's the fun in that?" She cut her eyes to mine.

A strange tingling fluttered at the tip of my fingers.

I rubbed my jaw. "You know what? I like you. Let's go."

I grabbed the tray of cups and motioned for her to follow me.

"Step one: get the vampires to like me, so I don't get eaten. Step two: show Theo what he's missing. Step three: profit."

"You missed a step. Step two is gathering your DNA. Then, we can show this Theo fellow who's boss." I pushed open the door behind the cellar and walked us down a short hallway before turning into the lab.

"Finn's not tested princess DNA. Come on. I'm curious. If I prick you, do you bleed rainbows?" I motioned for her to follow me.

"Ha! Now, that would be a fun party trick. No rainbows here, but I do have gold in my blood. It sparkles in the light. Don't you know? You were a prince once. I'm assuming you've been around your fair share of princesses."

"Not really. I never had the chance. Some princes don't get their happily ever after with a princess. You must not have paid attention in History class."

"Oh yeah? Well, you're absolutely right! History was boring! I'm not too ashamed to admit, I was too busy daydreaming and flunked out senior year. Besides, princess school wasn't like other schools. I hated lessons. Who wants to know how to summon a tree frog? Not me. I'd rather summon a dragon."

"I knew there was more to you than I thought, Princess." I nudged the door to the lab open with my shoulder.

A low hum escaped, echoing down the corridor. Penelope paused in the doorway.

"Come on. It's only machines and processors. We have a million things going on down here, but nothing that will harm you."

Except me, I thought.

I set the tray on a nearby table, checking over my shoulder to make sure she followed. She shuffled inside the room, taking in her surroundings. Her gaze fell to the blood cellar, where rows of labeled blood samples lined the shelves under a fog of cold vapor.

"What took so long?" Finn marched out of his office before stopping in his tracks at the sight of Penelope. "Princess." He threw his white coattails behind him and bowed.

"How did you—" she started.

"Finn, this is Princess Penelope. Princess, this is my brother and scientist, Finn. He studies everything and knows everything. I don't ask questions. Otherwise, he will go into an hour-long conversation, of which I'll understand nothing."

"Pleased to meet you," he said. "What brings you here, my lady?"

"I was told to be a lab rat." Penelope glanced at the hospital bed in the corner and twisted her arms behind her back.

"Interesting. Royal blood. That's not something I've had the pleasure of testing. I'm assuming you had to strike a deal for this one. But never mind that. It's not important. What's important is you being comfortable with us poking and prodding you a bit. Sounds more fun than it is." He winked.

"Are you sure you want to do this, Penelope?" I stepped into her, resting my hand on her lower back. Her warmth felt like sunshine against my palm.

"For the cause!" She swung her arm around, displaying her pulsating veins.

My fangs popped out again, pricking sharp against my lip, but Finn only laughed.

"Right this way, my lady." He pointed toward the sterile cot in the corner.

I'd lain there many times, getting IV drips, giving blood samples, and waiting to see if whatever meds he'd fed me would turn my toes pink or make my eyeballs melt. It wasn't fun, being the guinea pig. But for the end result—to feel the sun on my cheeks and breath in my lungs again—I was willing to do anything.

Penelope situated herself back on the cot while Finn began to work, tying a bandage tight around her arm and thumping her vein until it pulsed under the blinding halogen lights. I sat in a rolling chair beside her, squeezing her hand.

"I'm only taking a few vials. Lucky for you, that's all I need. I won't drain you today. And I'm definitely not mixing this with Project X. You'd be dead in a heartbeat. Vamps would tear down my doors to get more of you. Your blood is too special. I'll keep it up there at the top, on its high horse—er, chariot." He picked up the syringe.

"Ever been pricked before?" I asked, eyeing the needle.

"Have I? Of course! I'm no stranger to pain. I can handle it. I'm as tough as—"

"Just a little pinch and then …" Finn pushed the needle into the crook of her elbow, drawing out a stream of blood the color of a blazing autumn sun.

Penelope's eyes fluttered shut as her head rolled to the side, hanging in a limp and awkward angle.

"And then … she's out," I muttered, smoothing back her silken hair.

I couldn't look at her blood any longer. The mere sight of her golden pulse made my mouth water and my cock grow thick. I didn't know if I wanted to fuck her or drain her or both. I adjusted myself and fanned her cheeks, working on waking her back up.

"Oops. Guess we gave her a scare." Finn finished collecting her blood and pushed a cotton ball to her wound before wrapping it in another bandage.

"Do you think her blood will give us any clues? Know anything about princess DNA?" I asked, securing the bandage on her arm.

"Their powers are pretty useless—to us and anyone really. I'm doubtful, but it will be interesting to see what we can do with it. Maybe we can turn a frog into a prince or something. Command him to grow an army and fight The Council on our behalf," Finn snarled. "Or maybe her blood is poisonous. I'd serve them a glass of it one way or another if that were the case. Dirty bastards." Finn snatched up the vials of blood and disappeared to the lab.

I watched as he stomped around, shoving the blood samples into several machines. His wild, disheveled hair frayed around his pointed face, nearly hiding the jagged scar cutting across his right eyebrow. He never said how he'd received the scar. Like most vamps, we didn't like to discuss our past lives. Only Leo would ramble on about his time as a war lieutenant to gain authority over our small brotherhood. The rest of us preferred to forget the time before we died.

"Wake up, sunshine," I whispered in Penelope's ear.

"*Bibbidi boob*!" she sang before flinging herself upright on the bed, narrowly missing my head.

"Whoa! Not so fast! You'll pass out again." I steadied her wavering shoulders with my hands. Her nimble body felt as frail as a bird's bones under my massive hands.

"Where? What? Who? Did that pumpkin do this?" She rubbed her eyes.

"Uh, no. You're here on assignment. Now, let's get you something to eat and head to the ballroom. If you want to learn to be more princessy without your magic, then you've got a lot of work to do."

"Oh. Right." She pressed her fingertips to the bandage on her arm and cringed. "I'd rather not eat. Can we head straight to lessons? I'm already feeling pretty tired. What time is it anyway?"

"It's nearly midnight. You're on vamp time now. Come." I tugged at her wrists, lifting her off the bed.

She jumped into my arms, and just in time, my quick reflexes caught her in an embrace. Her entire body warmed beneath my touch.

"I'm not sure why I did that, but I'm going to take a wild guess that it wasn't very princessy. More along the lines of desperation. Ugh," she stammered, resting her head on my empty chest.

I shifted her higher, so her cheek lay on my shoulder instead of where a comforting heartbeat should exist.

"That'll work. Hang on." I gripped her tight and flew out of the room, racing through the quiet halls, up the cellar stairs, out the back door, across the barren lawn, and into the empty ballroom before she could protest.

"What. The. Fuck?" She wriggled out of my arms and slowly backed away, swaying back and forth. "If you ever do something like that again, Vail!" She pressed her fingertips to her temples.

"You'll what?" I asked, laughing. "Charm me with a permanent flower crown of daisies? Or perhaps you can sing and make my cheeks blush a rose color, like yours. I can't blush, you know. That'd be great."

"You!" She pointed at me and wrinkled her nose before becoming distracted by the golden arched windows, the red silken curtains, and the hand-etched murals decorating our twenty-five-foot ceiling. Our ballroom had been modeled after a famous royal court.

I inched closer to her.

She turned her attention back to me and stepped away.

"Almost." I smirked, stepping into her.

"Almost what?"

I gripped her in my arms and spun us around, arching her back. I dipped her as I had done with beautiful women in the past days of my life as a prince. Penelope's leg shot up in the air, causing her ruffled skirt to fall around her tapered hips. A hint of pink lace peeked out from underneath. She clung to me, hanging in my grasp like a rag doll—the exact reaction I'd hoped for.

"Almost have you so riled up, you'll stay on your toes. Lesson one," I whispered, my mouth inches from hers.

She stared at my fangs, her eyes half-lidded from under a thick row of lashes.

"I think I like being riled up." Her breath became heavy, purring against my lips.

I leaned in closer.

Crash!

I jerked us both upright and pushed her behind me, turning in the direction of the loud noise that had rudely interrupted my smooth moves. A large, bald, cat-like creature slid down the ballroom's floor-to-ceiling window, landing in a hard thump outside.

"Damn it, Otto!" Penelope groaned. Her heels echoed throughout the empty chamber as she stomped over to the window.

"What the hell was that?" I asked, following behind her.

"My gargoyle. He's as dumb as a rock. Probably thought you were attacking me and flew into the window."

"He hurt himself to distract me and save you? How sweet."

"No way. He flew into it because he's a dumbass and he didn't know it was a window." She put her forehead to the glass, cupped her palms around her face, and peered at the ground below.

"He's all right. He's moving. Let's finish this lesson. I think I liked that romantic dip." She pushed herself from the ledge and skipped to the middle of the ballroom.

I peered out the window, making sure the poor creature was indeed still alive. The gargoyle rolled onto his back, lifted his legs, and clawed at the air before stumbling to his feet. He pointed his claws at my eyes and then at his and back again.

Understood, I mouthed, nodding at the clumsy fellow. I turned away and glided back to Penelope.

"This room is gorgeous! Do you use it much?" Penelope twirled her skirt, circling the empty room while humming. Each hop she took sprouted a flower under her toes until a garden of wildflowers decorated her path.

"I would if I had someone as beautiful as you to dance with in it daily. Though I'm not sure the brothers would care for flowers in our showroom. This is where we entertain and bring in the big bucks, or so I hope. We haven't yet, but we're planning an investor ball soon. We desperately need the money to fund our research. I just have to talk Leo into it."

"A ball? I love balls! How exciting! Why wouldn't Leo want to throw a ball? Who doesn't like to party?" She swirled her skirt, sending a flutter of butterflies out from underneath.

"It could attract the wrong attention. Not everyone wants to cure vampirism, Princess." I smiled at her innocence, and yet I had a lingering feeling she was a lot less innocent than she pretended to be.

"I see." The flowers on her path wilted, disappearing in little puffs of pink clouds and confetti.

"But back to this event. It's why you're here in the ballroom. You're going to show off your princess skills in front of my guests, including Prince Theo."

She clasped her hands under her chin and squealed, bouncing on her heels. "How do I do that?"

"By pretending to be my fiancée and dazzling the crowd. Between your charm and mine, we're going to make a killing. Not literally, but you know. Everyone loves a romantic love story, and investors will flock to a power couple. My guests will be putty in your hands. A real-live princess is hard to come by these days."

"But I'm not very princessy." Her posture slumped, as if she'd already given up.

I gripped her shoulders in my hands and pulled her up, straightening her spine to full height. She lifted her chin, meeting my gaze.

"Now, you listen to me. You're absolutely breathtaking. Just because your spells aren't what they used to be doesn't mean you have no power. Besides, the butterfly trick was charming. What else are you hiding up there?"

"Dip me again like that, and you might find out." The corners of her mouth turned up into a grin.

"I knew you weren't so innocent. And I plan on it. Because lesson two is dance. This one will be easy for you though. I've seen the way you move." I walked to the side of the room and pushed a gold-plated button.

The middle of the painted ceiling creaked open, parting in a large gap. Penelope stared at the spectacle as our two-ton crystal chandelier lowered from the ceiling, filling the entire ballroom with a sparkling glow.

"Wow! That's brilliant! I can see it now. This will be the party of the year!" She clutched her chest and gave a long-drawn-out sigh. "Makes me miss my castle."

"So, we have a deal then? Think you can pretend to be mine for a night and dazzle my guests while we dazzle your ex–douche bag? We can kill two gargoyles with one stone." I cut my eyes to the window, where Otto stood, his chubby face plastered against the glass, smashing himself into an even odder shape. A string of drool escaped his whiskered mouth.

"We have a deal. But just pretending, right? Because I'm done with men!" She curled her hands into fists.

"Lucky for you, I'm not a man." I straightened my collar, brushing my wrists against my empty rib cage. It had been so long since I'd felt my heartbeat that I'd lost memory of the sensation.

"Okay, or a Prince Charming."

"Not that either. Sorry to break the bad news, but I'm more of a villain these days." I bowed to her before extending my hand.

"Then, we have a deal." She wrapped her warm palm around my icy fingertips and curtsied.

The tingling I'd felt earlier shot up my spine and settled into my chest. My once-forgotten heartbeat flooded back into my memory.

FIVE

PENELOPE

I RESTED MY HEAD against the window and watched the dead leaves drifting to the forest floor in a series of loops and swirls in the twilight. They danced in the wind, much like I'd danced with Vail in his luxurious ballroom a few nights ago. He spun us in circles, twisted me into pretzels, and even twirled me in the air. For a moment, I'd forgotten my reason for dancing and instead allowed myself to have fun.

Theo was no match for Vail's grace. Vail's royal blood shone as he performed, commanding the room—and me. With the flick of his wrist, he'd pulled me into him or pushed me away. His precise agility and quick reflexes reassured me he wouldn't let me stumble. I'd never known my body was capable of the smooth moves he taught me. I doubted, at the investor ball, all eyes would be on me. At least, not with him dazzling the crowd.

I blew a breath out through my nose, fogging up the glass. Outside, Otto and Trevor rolled around in the dirt.

The clever fox buried himself in a pile of leaves, camouflaging his reddish-orange fur with the colors of autumn. Otto being Otto stood, stupefied, as if his friend had disappeared entirely before his eyes. He tilted his head to the left, to the right, and to the sky, and he even searched under his foot. When Priscilla had sent me home with an enchanted gargoyle, I'd expected him to behave as a guardian, not add to my collection of useless things I had to take care of.

The clanging of pots and pans from the kitchen tore me from my trance, drawing my attention back to the task at hand.

"I'm coming!" I called out to my godmother. I pushed off the window ledge and danced into the kitchen, practicing my *one, two, three, one, two, three, three* steps Vail had insisted I learn.

"A lot of good you'll do now! It's almost finished!" Gertie opened the oven, letting a whiff of the roast beast out and causing my mouth to water.

The scent brought me back to my childhood when the hardest decision I'd had to make was if I wanted to braid my hair or let it hang loosely down my back. The life of a princess was as spoiled rotten as most people imagined. My sisters and I had never been expected to get our hands dirty, do manual labor, or involve ourselves in war. Our only tasks were to sing, charm, look pretty, and marry a prince. Without a prince, we were nothing. Never in the history of princesses had there been any turned to old crones—until me.

"Sorry! I was practicing my dancing, and then I sat down to rest and lost track of time. I would've helped if you'd asked!" I shuffled my feet to the kitchen table and poured a glass of Black Label.

Pumpkin rolled from the corner, stopping under my hoop skirt. I hopped back and kicked him, sending him flying across the wooden floor and back into his corner.

"You're the one who wanted to invite him over for dinner. It should be you in this hot kitchen, not me! I don't know why we never taught you princesses basic life skills and independence. If I could do it all over again, I'd do just that!" She shook her head and turned off the stove.

"You didn't have to do all this. He doesn't eat. I don't know why you want to go through all the trouble of impressing him. It's not like he's a prince I'm trying to marry!" I swirled my wine, dipping my nose into the glass and drawing a long breath.

"No. But maybe he knows someone available to save you. Goddess knows you can't save yourself." She curled a pair of pot holders in her fists and took the steaming meal from the oven.

"I can too!" I pulled out an old wooden chair and sat down, running my hand along the seat to check for splinters first. That was a lesson I'd learned upon moving to the cottage. A splinter in the ass was worse than an uncomfortable night of sleeping on an annoying pea.

"No, you can't! You crawl out of bed every morning, looking like death. I think you should've settled for the zombie at that old witch house because, lady, you're falling apart! I saw you undress today, and you had to pick up your boob and set it in your bra," Mirror Mirror called from the other side of the wall.

"I thought you were going to charm him to shut up! I can't have a rude mirror roasting my guest!" I balled my fists and glanced down at my chest to make sure my cleavage looked perky and perfect à la princess—not drooping and dragging à la whoever the hell I was these days.

"Mirror! Can you please keep your mouth shut, so I don't have to shut it for you? If you want back into a castle instead of this drab place, you'll be a part of the team. I don't want to die in this shack!" Gertie banged her palm on the wall, rattling Mirror Mirror on the other side.

"Pfft. Doubt that'll work. Maybe I should take him off the wall and lay him facedown in the basement. Cover him with blankets. Snuff him out." I took a long sip of wine.

"I heard that!" Mirror Mirror shouted.

Knock, knock, knock.

"He's here!" Godmother's eyes grew wide. She patted down her dress pockets, checking for her wand before barking orders. "Pumpkin, stay in your corner. Mirror Mirror, shut up. Penelope, you're up. Let's see how well you remember class and elegance. You can practice for your winery soiree. If we all become this vampire's dinner, it's on you. I'm stupidly putting my faith in you—and him. Don't fuck this up."

"Godmother! Where did you learn that language?" I put a hand to my ruffled collar.

"From you. Now, get the door. I'll pour the blood." Her voice drifted into a harsh whisper.

I stood up, smoothing my hands down my skirt and instantly regretting my big heart. I hadn't invited Vail to dinner to practice magic or charm. Nor had I asked him over because he had the body of a sculpted mid-century Viking and a voice that calmed and commanded me, all at once. I hadn't even invited him over because I was curious about sex with a vampire and if the rumors of mind-blowing ecstasy were true. I didn't plan on seducing him to find out.

Sure, I'd thought about it—a lot. In the bath, in the woods, when I was alone in bed and I was sure Mirror Mirror had fallen asleep. Vail had overtaken my fantasies ever since he whirled me around the ballroom and dipped me in the most romantic gesture I'd ever experienced. But every day I grew older, he stayed the same. The ex-prince vamp man and I would never work.

The real reason I'd invited him to dinner was to study him. He exuded an air of royalty and confidence that, no matter how hard I tried, I couldn't match. But even without my princessy qualities, at our last meeting, he'd treated me every bit of a queen.

I took a deep breath, swelling my bosom, and opened the door.

Vail stood, adjusting the lapels on his jacket. The tantalizing smell of his cologne drifted into my senses and caused me to let out a long, audible breath.

He froze, raking his eyes over my best ballgown, pausing his gaze at my puffed-out cleavage.

"My lady, you look exquisite." He bowed, licking his lips. A glint of fang shimmered beneath his smile.

"Thank you! Good evening. Come in!" My words spilled out in an unintelligible sentence that even I didn't understand.

Whatever grace and elegance I'd once had melted away at the sight of this vampire. He turned me into a royal shitshow.

Trevor and Otto circled Vail's feet, stopping him from entering the cottage. They sniffed his ankles, his polished loafers, his tight apple butt.

"You two! Stop that! Get!" I swatted the fox and gargoyle away.

Trevor growled, but Otto only gave a weird dance and went back to his pile of leaves.

"That's quite the friendly band of characters you've got there," Vail said as I ushered him inside and shut the door.

"Oh, that's just the start," I said in a singsong voice, accidentally stirring the duster in the corner. It lifted off the shelf and shook its feathers out before collapsing to the floor in a loud smack.

Vail raised an eyebrow.

"Good heavens, Princess! If you rose an octave, it might have actually done its job. I think your pitch might be off on that charm." Gertie peeked around the doorway, swallowing hard at the sight of Vail.

"You must be the beautiful lady's fairy godmother. I've heard so much about you." Vail took three long strides toward the kitchen and bowed in front of her.

"Vail, this is my godmother, Gertie. Gertie, this is my fake boyfriend and teacher of all things royal, Vail, the vampire." I nodded to them both.

"It's a pleasure to meet the man willing to take on this job. It's not for the faint of heart. But I think, between the two of us, we can get her back to where she belongs." Gertie bowed back, swishing her robes behind her.

"By the way she glided across the ballroom the other night, I'd say, she is well on her way." He smiled, showing a toothy grin.

"Ha-ha-ha!" Mirror Mirror cackled from the other side of the wall.

Vail looked from me to Gertie and back again.

A rush of heat crept up my neck, settling into my already-rosy cheeks.

"Oh, that's Mirror Mirror. He's having a bit of a hard time, adjusting to cottage life. Follow me. Might as well introduce you now and get on with the show." Gertie tugged at Vail's elbow, leading him into the bedroom.

"The shitshow," I muttered under my breath, following behind them.

Godmother opened the door to the dimly lit room and cut her eyes to Mirror Mirror.

"This is our enchanted mirror. Mirror Mirror, this is our guest, Vail. He's one hundred percent vampire and one hundred percent—" Gertie said.

"Delicious! Whatever is a man like you doing in a rat hole like this? Are you unwell?" Mirror Mirror's mouth hung open, fogging up his entire face.

"I was going to say one hundred percent a gentleman, so you knew to behave, but I'm sure he's flattered." Godmother sighed.

"Undoubtedly. And you'll know I am one hundred percent certain I'm not unwell. I'd like to think I'm the lucky one in the company of such beauty and entertainment tonight. Thank you for the invite, Penelope." Vail turned toward me.

I dipped my head and stared at my worn leather boots.

"Oh, her. Well, did you know—" Mirror Mirror started.

Gertie pulled her wand out and pointed it at the mirror, turning him into a nude painting, complete with old man balls.

Vail drew a sharp breath.

"Don't worry. It'll only last until morning. Perhaps we might get some sleep tonight instead of hearing his yakking. I think he'll be nicer once he's settled into a familiar environment again. This cottage hasn't been good for any of us." Gertie swirled around and tipped her head back toward the kitchen. "Let's eat!"

"I think the cottage is quite charming … and warm. It feels much different here than back at home, where the halls are cold and empty." Vail's voice trailed off. He stepped aside, letting me pass.

"You mean, you'd give up grand rooms, stately offices, three-storied libraries, and the security of a castle for"—I motioned to the crumbling walls inside my house—"this?"

"I didn't say I'd give up a castle! I only spoke of the winery. It's not my ideal place to call home." Vail pulled a chair out from under the table and motioned for me to sit before sitting across from me.

"Where did you call home?" Gertie asked, gently pushing a wineglass filled with thick, inky blood toward him.

She'd managed to buy the blood from Priscilla earlier. The virgin blood was of the highest quality, according to the witch. The poor maiden who had been drained was a love-struck young lady who wandered into the wrong shop one day, where Drake awaited with his charm.

Vail peered into the glass and took a deep breath. His eyes fluttered back before he took a sip.

"Favola." He licked his lips.

"Favola. I've heard of that city! I remember a bit of dark history there. I always thought the vampire rumors were hogwash. But … are you—" Gertie tapped a finger to her chin.

"Prince Valerian. I disappeared at age twenty-eight after vampires massacred my kingdom. The Roman Catholic Church worked with The Council back then, as they probably do now. I don't know. I left the royal life and traveled for centuries, finally settling here in Morningwood. So, I guess you could say we have that in common, save for a few hundred years." He tossed his head back, taking a long gulp of blood. His cool demeanor changed with each sip as he loosened up.

"I'm so sorry. I had no idea. I never learned anything about it." I reached for his hand resting on the table and squeezed it. His cold skin went clammy.

"I didn't mean to bring that up. I'm very sorry about what happened to you. Penelope doesn't know these things. She wasn't ever taught them. It's a disservice not to teach princesses the ways of the world, but no one asked me. I do what I'm told. When she bloomed, I never knew the trouble I was in for." Gertie huffed. She set the roast on the table and began carving slices of meat off the bone, putting it on a plate and shoving it toward me.

"Who? Penelope? Trouble? Nah." Vail laughed, displaying a set of crimson-stained fangs.

I wondered if vampires could get drunk on blood like I'd gotten drunk on his wine many, many times. The Black Label varietal snuck up on me before I had the chance to slow down. The last time I'd downed an entire bottle, I had woken up in the bathtub in my wedding dress. My eyes had nearly been swollen shut from crying, and both Trevor and Pumpkin had moaned beside me—Trevor because he thought I was dead and Pumpkin because he liked the sight of me soaking wet and drunk.

I narrowed my eyes at Pumpkin, who sat curiously quiet across the room. He took my gaze as a signal to roll under our feet, playfully nudging Vail's leg. I promptly kicked the butterball away.

"Pervy enchanted pumpkin, heh." I shrugged, piercing a slice of roast with my fork.

Vail craned his neck, looking toward Pumpkin's corner. The big orange goof wiggled his drawn-on brows.

"Yes, trouble. The lot of 'em." Gertie plopped herself in a chair and began to eat.

"I'm not trouble. I'm only experiencing a mild setback." I cut my eyes to Godmother.

"And one we're working on fixing. You know, Gertie, I think you've done an amazing job with Penelope. When we first met, she sang like a bird. And the other night, when we danced, she flew across the floor as if she had wings. I'd say whatever's going on with her magic might well be on its way out. She seems like a proper, charming princess to me." Vail finished his glass of blood and reached for the pitcher to pour another.

"Thank you, Vail," Godmother said. A hint of color flashed across her pale, washed-out cheekbones.

"You *are* a Prince Charming. Is that the blood talking?" I took a sip of wine, peering at him over the rim of the glass.

"Not at all. It's the truth." He situated his legs under the table, brushing one against mine.

"She certainly is special. I knew it before I picked her. All the other fairy godmothers wanted the rose or the peony. But I waited at the Princess Patch for the sunflower. Once she bloomed, I claimed her as mine. Turns out, Princess Francine, of the rose, is a real brat anyway. She's been through four fairy godmothers, last I heard. Not sure how a prince will put up with that one."

"Princess Penelope, born of the sunflower? That would have been my first guess too. Perhaps that's why I feel a bit of warmth on my skin when I'm near you. You're like sunlight without the potential to kill me." He leaned forward on his elbows.

"Don't underestimate me." I scrunched my brows, trying my best to appear menacing.

But a ladybug flew out from behind my ear and landed on the tip of his nose.

I covered my mouth with my hand and giggled.

"I'll be sure to watch my back with you," he said, plucking the bug off and setting it down on a withering bouquet in the center of the table.

"You'd better. I—" I dropped my glass on the table, spilling the last few drops of my wine. My head spun as what felt like little electric shocks zapped in my brain. I shut my eyes tight and didn't open them again until my world stopped spinning.

The heavy scent of cooking grease hung in the air of a diner I'd only whirled by briefly a handful of times before.

"Um, where did you come from?" a woman asked, sitting in the booth across from me. She sat with her palms wrapped around a giant mug of brown liquid on the table. A half-eaten piece of dry toast lay in a pile of crumbs on a plate beside her. In front of me was a notebook, a pencil, and a newspaper.

I ran my fingers along the paper, blackening them with ink. I hadn't seen a newspaper since I left Poppycock. Theo used to have them brought in special from the human world. The written word was the only thing connecting the dimensions. We would both sit and read the papers in the morning, confused about most things the other side reported. We didn't have anything like it in our world. The news only traveled by word of mouth, carrier animals, or magic.

"Hello?" the woman asked again, tilting her head to get a better look at me.

I lifted my gaze to hers.

"Where am I?" I asked, raising my voice over the clinking of dishes as a woman began cleaning the table next to us.

Her stained pink apron hung, barely tied around her wide hips. She scrubbed her dishrag against the table, knocking off bits of bread crust and what looked like egg. She tossed the rag over her shoulder and plucked a green piece of paper from between two glass jars, stuffing the parchment in her pocket.

"You're at The Royal Beagle. Are you okay? You've got red across your corset. It looks like wine, but there's no telling in this town. I'm guessing you aren't from around here." The lady pushed her mug aside and leaned forward.

"I'm … I'm …" I shifted my eyes to the surrounding tables.

A group of older people sat in the corner, laughing. One man took out a handkerchief and blew his nose right over his plate of food.

I flinched.

"I'm not from here. I think I might be … lost. And unwell." I shifted in my seat, pressing my heel into a sticky spot on the floor. Nausea bubbled inside my stomach.

A door swung open with the ringing of a bell and a blast of outside traffic noise, startling me further into the booth.

"Here. Drink this." She took her mug and scooted it across the table toward me.

"You want me to drink that muddy water? No offense, lady, but it looks like it came from a chamber pot."

"It's coffee. Trust me, it will make you feel alive. You look like you've traveled far. Like maybe from a different world." She grabbed the pencil and scribbled something down in her notebook.

"Well, would that make me crazy if I said I did?" I took her mug and sniffed it. The aroma alone awakened my senses, filling me with a comforting warmth. I gulped the hot liquid down and let out an audible, "Ahhh."

The lady smirked.

"Lucky for you, you appeared before the only person around here who wouldn't think you were crazy." She chewed the end of her pencil and narrowed her eyes before scribbling down more notes.

"How so?" I asked, taking another sip of coffee. The drink worked like magic. I instantly felt better.

"I've been to the supernatural realm and back again." She swatted a fly from her plate.

"You know about magic?" My eyes widened. "But you're human. How can that be?"

"I'm Fritzi Cox," she said, reaching out and spinning the newspaper around so it faced me.

I read the words in small print at the bottom.

MORNINGWOOD MAGIC:
FAIRY TALES FROM THE
WORLD'S MOST HAUNTED CITY

BY FRITZI COX

"I don't understand," I stammered. "How do you know about where I'm from?"

"I don't exactly. I know some things. As I said, I've been to your dimension before. But I've no clue who you are."

"I'm Princess Penelope." I dropped my head, ashamed to utter my own name these days. I didn't feel like a princess, and now that I was in the human world, I wasn't sure I could call myself one anymore.

"A princess!" Fritzi shouted, putting her hand to her mouth.

The diner quieted for a moment before the guests were bored with us and began picking at their food again.

"I think. Or I used to be." I slumped in my seat.

"Go on." Fritzi put her pencil to her notepad again, jotting down words in messy scribbles I couldn't decipher.

I put down the empty mug and stared into it as I bit my lip. I'd never stayed in the human world this long. Usually, I'd pass by this dimension in a blur of memories that I couldn't piece together or understand. I had to get back home to Godmother, or she'd be worried sick.

I shivered, sliding my palms up and down my prickled arms.

The woman in the apron rushed by our table, pausing to fill up the cup with more magic brown water.

I perked, taking the mug between my palms and inhaling the steam. I took a long, slow sip of coffee and settled into my seat.

"Once upon a time," I sighed.

SIX

VAIL

I JERKED TO MY feet, knocking my chair to the floor, when Penelope disappeared in a puff of pink glitter.

"Where is she? Is this some kind of trick?" I shouted, glancing behind me and around the room for whatever fool thought it would be fun to play with a vampire.

Pumpkin quickly rolled away, stashing himself in a broom closet.

"She's gone. It's her fading in and out again. She never knows where she goes, but she's usually back in a flash." Gertie drew her wand and held it, pointed at me. "This isn't my doing, and there's nothing you can do about it. Just sit and wait. Don't go baring those fangs at me!"

I held my hands in the air, showing her my palms. "I don't mean you any harm. It caught me off guard, is all. I don't like the look she had on her face. She looked as if she was in a good deal of pain." I paced the floor, nearly tripping over the uneven cobblestones that had settled with age.

"Traveling dimensions will do that. Ever met a time traveler?" She lowered her wand to the table but still held it curled in her fist. The loose skin across her knuckles pulled tight, whitening with her grip.

"No. Is that what she is?" I stared out the window above the kitchen sink and into a pitch-black void. The moon had disappeared too.

"I don't think so. As far as I can tell, she only pops into the human world, I guess. Once, she said she saw cars racing down a street that looked like ours, except she said it was much, much busier. I can't help much. I don't deal with humans. But you …" Her voice trailed off.

"I'll do whatever it takes." I turned on my heels, peering straight at her.

"Priscilla mentioned your labs were working on other things besides curing vampirism. You have Penelope's blood. Maybe you can figure out how to cure her too. She's like my daughter even if she's not of my blood. When this happens, I never know if I'll see her again. It's become more frequent. I know, one day, she won't come back. Please, help her. I don't know what else to do."

She let go of her wand and rested her head in her hands, rubbing her temples in a circular motion. Her silver hair frayed out like a cotton ball, framing her tired face.

I walked back to my chair, picked it up, and sat down in front of her. "I'm going to stay here until she gets back, and after she rests, it's back to the labs. We'll figure it out. You have my word."

"How can I trust a vampire?"

"You can't. But I don't think you have a choice." I plucked Penelope's empty wineglass off the table and filled it before pushing it toward the old lady.

We sat in the kitchen until close to midnight, chatting about her predicament. Gertie said the princess's magic began to fade after Theo proposed but took a turn for the worse when he left her at the altar. Penelope had never shared the details with me, and after hearing the story from her godmother, I was happy she never mentioned it. The thought of someone breaking her brought out the beast in me. The entire time Gertie spoke of the wedding, my fangs dripped with the bitter toxin I hadn't used in years.

"So, he never even said anything? He just wrote her a letter and sent her away? On her wedding day?" My nostrils flared.

"Yes. She was no longer of use to him once her powers faded. He was ashamed of her failures and took them as a reflection on himself." She put her hand to her mouth and stifled a yawn.

"That bastard needs more than regret. Perhaps I can arrange—"

Poof!

Penelope appeared in her chair, tumbling backward and smacking her head on the cobblestone.

Gertie and I rushed to her side, helping the princess to her feet.

"This back and forth is going to kill me one day," Penelope muttered, rubbing the back of her head.

"Are you all right? Are you hurt? Why were you gone so long that time?" Gertie's voice rose to a screeching level.

"Yes. I'm okay. I think. I'm confused, is all, and maybe a little dizzy." Penelope swayed, collapsing into my arms. She smelled of bacon grease and toast.

"Sit down. I'll make you some tea." Gertie rushed to the cupboard and pulled out an antique silver kettle.

I eased the princess down into her seat. Her body trembled under my hands.

"Tea." Penelope scrunched her nose. "I wish I had magic bean water."

Gertie looked from me to the princess and back again. I shrugged my shoulders before brushing my hand over the back of Penelope's head, checking for a lump.

"Magic bean water? Don't tell me you're trying to grow a beanstalk again. What do you need that for? Where were you just then?" Gertie asked, setting the kettle on the stove. She turned the knob, lighting the boiler's fire in a *flumph*.

"It was called The Royal Beagle. I drank some potion that was brown and looked completely unappetizing. But it made me feel alive. Maybe you should try it." She looked at me.

"I know The Royal Beagle. But brown water? Do you mean coffee?" I asked. I brought my chair around the table and sat next to her, keeping her close.

"Yes! Coffee! That's it." Her voice shook. Her familiar rosy hue had turned clammy and pale.

"I don't know anything about that magic. But this tea will fix you right up. Then, you can tell us all about your travels," Gertie said.

Otto and Trevor pawed at the door.

"I think I need to lie down, Godmother. I don't have much to say. I only sat in a diner and drank the coffee." She pushed herself up from the table and looked away.

"Let me help you!" I stood up, grabbing her elbow to steady her.

"Thanks. Can you let my fox in? And I guess that dumb gargoyle. They're used to sleeping with me."

"Of course." I disappeared to the front room, creaking the door open to let the creatures inside.

They rushed off, stumbling over each other. I followed them until I reached the kitchen. The sight of Penelope holding her godmother in a weak embrace stopped me in my tracks. I paused, leaning against the doorway.

"Love you, Godmother. I'll talk in the morning. I don't feel very well right now."

"That's all right, dear. Get some rest." Gertie kissed the top of her head before holding her at arm's length. "I'm glad you're back safe."

"Me too." Penelope shuffled her feet out of the kitchen, giving me a lazy half-smile as she passed.

Gertie turned her watery gaze back to the stove.

"Do you need help? Can I walk you to bed? Are you sure you can make it?" I asked.

She moved at a snail's pace down the hall and toward her room, waving me off. Trevor circled her feet, and then the clever fox leaned himself against her leg, as if he could keep her from toppling over. Otto scooted his butt across the floor behind them.

"Thanks, Vail. I appreciate it. But I don't need a man. I can take care of myself," she grumbled, disappearing into her room.

I rubbed the back of my neck, fighting off the instinct to rush to her side, as if I somehow knew her better than she knew herself. But I had an inkling I did.

"She lies, you know. She does need someone. A man, woman, me. She's a princess. Poor thing was never taught how to take care of herself, though she tries. Stubborn girl." Gertie clicked her tongue. "That's why I'm doing my best to teach her now. But it's hard to teach an old dog new tricks." She sighed.

I stretched my arms over my head, barely missing the rafters tucked in the low ceiling. The cottage had seemed much smaller, darker, and desperate after Penelope's disappearance. I fixated my sleepy stare on a spider busying himself in a tangle of cobwebs stuck alongside the corner of a wooden beam.

"Don't worry, Gertie. I'll help. We'll get her on her feet in no time. After all, I have all the time in the world," I said, readying myself to leave.

"But she doesn't." She scrubbed her palms across her tired eyes before lifting her gaze to mine.

I'd never seen someone look so miserably defeated in all my centuries.

She drew her attention back to the stove, where the kettle began to whistle, sputtering out a cloud of steam into the sudden chill hanging in the air. The tingling warmth that radiated from Penelope had disappeared with her.

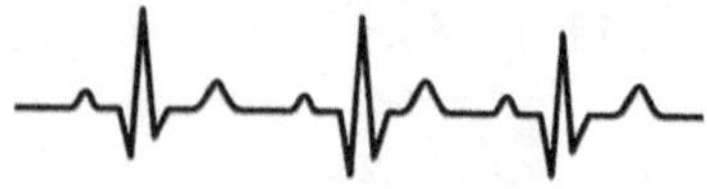

I hadn't slept much over the last few days. Every night, I'd wait for a message from Otto or Penelope's knock at my door. And each night, I was met with either silence or the comforting company of my brothers. Finn rarely emerged from the basement. Lately, he'd been spending so much time in the lab that he slept down there, passing out on the old cot well after dawn.

Ian stayed busy in the barn, and Drake was never at home. The only two vampires around these days were Leo and me. We both worked tirelessly, ushering humans in and out of our winery, all while collecting their DNA samples right under their noses.

"I'm telling you, I don't think it's a good idea. We'll draw the wrong attention." Leo's voice came out as gruff and scruffy as his signature scraggly beard. The old vampire was set in his archaic and overly masculine ways.

"We have about two weeks of financials left before this place gets shut down. We simply can't survive unless we bring in investors. Priscilla has done all she can. Antonio and the pack too. Besides, they'll all be here. They'll only put the word out through trustworthy sources." I wiped the bar down, setting the tray of fresh samples aside.

"Like your princess?" He raised his brows. "She knows far too much."

"We can trust her. She's working with us … and she's helping with the investor ball. Maybe next time she's here, you can get to know her a bit. Her bubbly personality will grow on you. You could use some softening up, old man."

"I thought she was only a lab rat," he said, loosening the strings on a trash bag and stuffing it with another empty bottle.

"She's not *just* a lab rat. She's a lot more than that! She's helping, just like the wolves and just like the witches. She's a part of the team," I said.

Leo studied me in silence before speaking again. A slow smile built across his bloodstained lips. He'd helped himself to Project X after an incredibly tempting woman flirted with him all night during the wine tasting. If any vampire had self-control, it was our dear leader, Leo.

"More than a lab rat. You're feeling something. Did Finn inject you with her blood? Did you drink from Penelope?" He tied the string on the trash bag and swiftly came toward me, resting the back of his palm to my forehead.

I drew in a long breath and swatted it away. "I'm not warm. And, no, he didn't. I've not heard from him—or her—for nearly a week."

"You're not warm, but you're different. I can tell. You should be down there with Finn now, getting monitored. I think whatever experiment he put you through might be onto something."

"He hasn't done anything to me lately."

"Then, it's not him. It's all her. Get her back here for testing, stat," he said, picking up the rest of the trash and heading upstairs.

I gathered the tray of spit cups and made my way toward the lab. I hadn't told Leo about the warm flush I felt around Penelope because I knew this would happen. The brothers would have her in the lab, hooked up to ten different monitors and caged like a bird. If they knew this princess could hold the key to our future, they'd never let her leave Bostwick.

I put my back against the swinging lab door and pushed it open. The rush of cold air hit me in the face faster than Penelope did, knocking me back into the wall and spilling our samples down the front of her dress.

"Penelope!" I cringed at the red sludge dripping down her heaving chest. "What're you doing here?"

She held her hands out, shaking drops of spit from her fingertips and shrieking, "Get it off me! Get it off! This is disgusting!" She gagged.

"What's going on?" Finn stepped out of his office, surveying the damage to Penelope and his samples.

"An accident. I'm afraid this one is a lost cause." I opened the cabinets on a nearby cupboard and searched for something to clean her up with.

"I'm not a lost cause!" Penelope huffed, still scrunching her nose. She stood frozen in place, as if she thought moving might make her ickier.

"Not you! I meant, the samples." I grabbed a roll of paper towels from a shelf and nodded toward the spilled cups.

"I'll clean it. I'll clean it." Finn rushed to my side, plucking the towels from my hand.

"Sorry, brother. I wasn't expecting company. I didn't know I would be running into a princess this evening. To what do I owe the honor?"

She still stood, immobile, pouting at her ruined dress.

Finn tore a paper towel from the roll and handed it to me. I wiped the spit from the front of her corset, brushing my hand against her in rough, jerking movements. Her breasts jiggled softly with each swipe of my hand. My fangs began to ache.

"I wasn't either. But I tested her blood today and had a bit of a breakthrough. So, I got Drake to bring her back." Finn took a handful of paper towels to the trash bin and dropped them in.

"Drake? Why didn't you ask me?" I asked, pausing before I finished cleaning the spit off of Penelope's breasts.

"You were with guests. In the tasting. It's all good now. I got what I needed. Did you know Penelope runs hot? Her natural temperature is slightly above a human's."

"Jeez. You two talk about me like I'm not even here. Whatever. Look, I'm tired. I came here to give him what he needed and to get what I needed—which is you. Now, stop mopping drool off my chest, and let's dance."

Finn raised his eyebrows and pivoted on his heels, returning to the lab.

I tossed the dirty paper towel in the trash before grabbing her and spinning us around. She quickly fell in line with my rhythm, grinding her hips into mine as we glided across the lab in a whirl of wine-and-spit-stained romance.

"One, two, three. One, two, three, three. Someone's been practicing." I smiled, holding her against me. Her heartbeat raced against my empty chest.

"Of course I have. Gotta show my ex what he's missing," she said, breathless.

"And then what?"

"What do you mean, and then what?"

"What will you do after you've proven yourself to him?"

She glanced down, scuffing her foot across the floor before looking away.

"I haven't gotten that far yet." She slouched, avoiding my gaze.

"Will you go back if he apologizes?"

"No."

"What if he begs?"

"No."

"Grovels?"

"Maybe."

I clasped her trembling chin between my fingers and lifted her eyes to mine.

"No, you won't. You're Princess Penelope. And you don't need a man." I snapped my fingers in the air and bobbed my head—a move I'd seen Priscilla do countless times when speaking of her ex-husbands.

Penelope laughed, clutching her sides. The strings on her corset loosened with each deep breath she took.

"I only need dance lessons. And maybe a little wine." She twirled, grabbing a nearby bottle and dancing out of the room.

"To the ballroom!" I shouted, swooping her into my arms and whisking her away.

Her petite body radiated more energy than it had the last time I saw her.

She curled her arms around the bottle, clutching the wine instead of me.

"Off we go!" She cracked an invisible whip in the air.

I took off, hurdling over obstacles and through the halls. I swept past Drake, two werewolves, and a goat. Penelope squealed, reaching out to run her hand along the goat as we passed by in a flash before we made it to the ballroom.

"What's he doing here?" she asked.

"That's Grump. He showed up last week and hasn't left yet. He's no bother. Grump only roams around, grazing all day. A couple of times, we found his head in a bucket of fermented grapes. When Ian went to take it away, the goat head-butted him, stumbled left, stumbled right, and then passed out with all four legs in the air. He's a grumpy little thing. Hence the name. Ian gives him a bucket of wine now. Probably why he won't leave."

Penelope pulled herself up, peering over my shoulder at the goat we'd left behind. "He's following us!"

I stopped, turning around to see the drunk goat running toward us on legs that didn't seem to work together. "Ah, well, let him. He can watch. Our first guest that we have to dazzle, my lady. I'm afraid he can't offer commentary, but …"

"Think again," said Grump, catching up to us.

"You can talk!" I shouted, nearly dropping Penelope.

"Ah. Is that what I'm doing? I thought I was out in the pasture with the beer shits." The goat swayed before falling over on its side.

"Wow. A rude, real-life enchanted goat." Penelope's mouth dropped.

Grump held a hoof in the air. "You forgot drunk."

"I think you found your spirit animal," I said.

"Vail Bostwick! How dare you insult me by comparing me to this … this …"

Grump hopped to his feet, sobbing. He let out a bloodcurdling scream before falling over again and snoring loudly.

"Shit. That's me." Penelope unscrewed the cap on the wine and took a swig straight from the bottle. She wiped her forearm across her mouth.

"Let's go. I've had enough drama for the night. He can sleep out here. I'd much rather be dancing with a beautiful princess than staring at an inebriated goat." I clutched her to my chest as we made our way into the ballroom.

She reached out, flicking on the chandelier button as we passed it.

"This feels like home," she said, hopping from my arms and setting the bottle of wine on a table. She twirled around with her hands held out. Her skirt whistled in birdsong as she flew around the dance floor.

I stood, transfixed on the subtle glow she put out when she was here, in her element. She skipped around the room, twirling out butterflies and glitter. At one point, I thought I'd caught a bat escaping out from under her skirt, but she never skipped a beat. She kept on dancing until she reached me.

"You do seem to come alive at the luxurious side of life," I said.

"I miss it. The parties especially. There was cake and confetti and gifts and flowers and …" She stopped in front of me, peering down at her feet. "Like a wedding."

I lifted her chin with my fingertips. "Chin up. Every time you start to spiral into this funk, you look down. Quit looking down. You're going up. Not down. Don't look at your feet."

"Right. Don't look at my feet. Got it." She took a deep breath.

I bowed to her, extending my hand. "Now, may I have this dance, future fake bride of Bostwick?"

She flashed me a smile, instantly sending a warm tingle up my spine and into my lips.

"I thought you'd never ask." She curtsied, bending down low enough for me to catch an appetizing glimpse of her cleavage, still sticky with the residue from the spilled samples.

I took her hand in mine and placed my other hand around her back before steering us across the room. Her pulse quickened under my fingertips. I felt her rapid heartbeat through her clothes.

"One, two, three. One, two, three, three," I whispered, my senses coming alive, the longer I held her.

Her eyes shot down to her feet again. A flush of pink crept into her cheeks.

"Uh-uh-uh! Eyes on mine. I won't let you fall." I jerked her arm, gaining her attention back to me.

"One, two, three. One, two, three, three," she repeated, watching her reflection in my dilated eyes. The vein in her neck pulsed with each breath she took as she counted over and over again.

I twirled her out from me and pulled her back in, close enough to smell the sunlight still left on her skin from earlier. I imagined her dancing in the clearing in the forest, the sun warming her face. I grasped her against me, sliding my hands down her hips and molding her to me. I forcefully matched her movements to mine, keeping our rhythm in sync. My cock thickened against my thigh.

She looked to her feet again before catching herself and quickly looking back up.

Her heartbeat became deafening to my ears. My fangs ached with blinding pain. I needed to bite.

I stopped mid-stride, dropping her arms from me and stepping away.

"What is it?" she asked.

I bared my fangs and took a deep breath.

She gasped, leaving her lips slightly parted and showing me a glimpse inside her wet mouth. My dick strained against my slacks.

"I can't help it, Penny. I'm a vampire. Sometimes, I need to bite. And you … you're the most delicious damn thing I've ever encountered. You feel like sunlight, you smell like sunlight, and I'm going to take a wild guess that you taste like it too. I don't know who's more dangerous—you or me." I ran my hands through my hair, turning from her to gather myself.

My fists curled tight as she clasped her palm on my shoulder and tugged me back around. Her fingertips blazed a trail across my shoulder and down my chest, as if she'd raked hot coal against my skin. Her finger curled under the button on my slacks. "Bite me, and let's see." She pulled me toward her.

I grew hot. Feverish.

"I can't. You don't—you have no idea what kind of door you'd open if you let me do that." I gritted my teeth, fixating on the pulse erratically beating above her collar.

"I don't want to open doors. I want to smash windows and break down walls. I need it just as much as you. Bite me." She shoved her wrist in my face. Her chest rose and fell with each heavy breath she took.

I threaded my fingers with hers, pulling her wrist to my lips and inhaling. Her flesh prickled at my touch. One bite of Penelope, and I'd become unchained and unable to focus on our task. But when a princess gave me a command, like a true Prince Charming, I obeyed.

I licked the goose-bumped flesh below her palm. She arched her head back and exhaled a soft moan. Her heartbeat played across my tongue in the same rhythm we'd repeated earlier.

One, two, three. One, two, three, three.

I hissed, sinking my fangs into skin. She flinched before pushing her wrist deeper into my mouth. Her heat seared across my lips, satisfying a need I suppressed all too often.

I sucked her sweet nectar down my throat, drunken with the taste of her that I could only describe as *bright*. I could feel her blood traveling slowly throughout me, lighting me from the inside and warming my dead body in a feeling I'd forgotten long ago. Her pulse was mine.

She jerked her arm away, pulling me out of my trance. My fangs were still bared, and a slight dribble of blood dripped from my lip. I shook my head and wiped it away.

"You aren't giving me that toxin, right? When I said bite me, I meant, just eat a little! Not turn me into a vamp!" She pressed her palm to her wrist, squeezing it. Her eyes studied mine.

I pulled off my jacket, ripped my buttons down, and tore off my shirt. I wrapped the cloth around her wrist and held it tight before answering.

Fuck, she mouthed, taking in my naked chest. "I mean … wow. I'm losing my class. I'm trying to compliment you. You look amazing! On second thought, I don't mind if you bite me again. Does it taste different from other areas?" She brushed her fingers against her inner thigh.

"Thank you. No toxins. No more bites. And, yes, on the taste." I winked. "Though it's not the taste so much as it is more of a mental thing. I only bite the necks or wrists of prey. And I only bite other areas for particular needs."

I fumbled with the shirt, tying it around her wrist in a makeshift bandage. Her blood still sparked in me, tingling me alight, as if I glowed with sunshine from the inside, but my skin was still cold to the touch as I ran my palm up my arm.

"I see," she said, glancing down at her feet again.

"Ahem." I cleared my throat.

She lifted her gaze to mine.

"What did I tell you about looking down? We're going up. Or … you're going up. Up there actually." I jerked my head toward the chandelier, quickly changing the subject. A flicker—or heartbeat—thumped under my skin before fading. I rubbed the back of my neck and took a step back.

I wanted nothing more than to taste below Penelope's collar or the spot where her ass curved into her inner thigh. I'd love to suck on her breasts or tease her clit with my nose while I nibbled between her legs.

But her addictive blood bubbled inside me like a terrifying curse, confirming my suspicions. I knew Penelope was more than a lab rat. She was the cure.

SEVEN

PENELOPE

I STRETCHED OUT ON the lumpy couch in front of the fireplace, propping my feet on Trevor and using him as a pillow. My crystal slippers had rubbed blisters across my ankles after countless nights spent dancing at the winery. Vail and I had danced from midnight to dawn three times this past week until I finally declared I needed a break. Every part of my overspent body ached.

I held my wrist up, turning it in the firelight and inspecting the blue shadow that veiled two tiny blood marks. Vail had fed from me twice. The first time, I stubbornly pushed him to bite me. But the second time, he didn't even ask. I jumped into his arms and pressed my wrist to his lips the moment he told me Theo RSVP'd to the investor ball. He smirked before baring his fangs and digging in. Knowing he could release his toxin in me at any moment sent an exhilarating rush of danger from my head, straight down to my *royal flower.*

Being the gentleman he was, Vail stopped himself before becoming carried away but not before I saw his bulge below the belt. The longer he held my wrist to his lips, the longer his *magic wand* grew under his slacks. I'd thought back to the dark curse I'd placed on Theo long ago after I first left the kingdom. I had come across a spell to grow his nose hairs faster than he could keep up with them.

I wondered, *If I can make nose hairs grow like weeds, what else can I charm to become bigger?*

I threw my head back and laughed, startling Otto, who was lying on the floor beneath me, snoozing a whistling sound from his nose. He popped his head over the edge of my frayed, lumpy couch and growled.

"Lie back down. It's just me." I waved him away and took another sip of wine before reaching over and pouring the rest in Grump's bowl.

I hadn't planned on bringing the old goat home from the winery, but after I'd met him the first night, he had come back the next night to see me too. With each twirl, spin, or dip at Vail's hand, Grump would provide drunken commentary. After the goat had given my dismount from the chandelier a score of ten and praised my tango skills in between hiccups, I'd let the pathetic beast follow me home. Grump was the opposite of Mirror Mirror, and I could use a lot more encouragement in my life.

I slammed my spell book shut and set it aside. Rain pelted against the windows of the cottage all day and all night, keeping me holed up inside instead of outside, dancing among the falling leaves. Godmother had made me rest anyway.

Yesterday, I'd revisited Fritzi. I'd been minding my own business, practicing my singing in Mirror Mirror, much to his dismay, when I poofed out of my room and back into the diner. It was just after lunch when I felt the familiar zaps pulling me toward the other realm.

I didn't try to stop it this time. I only took a deep breath, braced myself for the ride, and murmured a quick, "Be right back," to my horror-stricken godmother.

And just like last time, I spent far too long sipping magic bean juice and discussing my life with my makeshift human therapist, Fritzi. She told me a little of her world, and I told her all of mine. I wasn't exactly sure what made me comfortable enough to offer her top-secret information on Bostwick, but there was something about the lady who I knew could one day help me in return.

After our deep conversations, I stayed in her world long enough to eat a slice of pie and stroll down the avenue, admiring every curiosity I passed, much to my new friend's assistance. She pointed out things she knew were only a part of her world, such as bicycles. Why anyone would want to straddle that contraption and huff and puff their way to a destination was beyond me. I asked her about horse-drawn carriages, but she only looked at me in disbelief. I told her about my adventures with the car, but right before we made it across the street to her car, I zapped back home again. Gertie had fallen asleep at the kitchen table.

I didn't tell Gertie or anyone about my human friend. I'd decided before returning home to save any trouble for all of us; it was better not to divulge secrets between the worlds. Fritzi had promised to protect my life by changing any names in any reporting, and I'd promised not to mention her to the Bostwick brothers.

A chill struck me across my cheeks. The draft from the cracked windows nearly blew out the fire.

"*La-la-la-la-la-la, muah!*" I sang, blowing a kiss toward the fireplace to hopefully ignite its smoldering embers.

A puff of ashes shot out from the hearth in a loud, rude noise before covering the floor in a thin dusting of soot.

"I give it a three out of ten," Grump said, taking another gulp from his bucket.

I sighed, grabbed the bottle of wine, and drank from it straight. The alcohol warmed my throat and settled into my belly, lulling me into slumber. I slept through the entire evening, only waking at the sound of my godmother making breakfast the next morning.

I rolled off the couch, wrapped myself in a blanket, and let the animals out before shuffling my feet toward the kitchen. The scent of Gertie's raspberry scones tickled my nose, causing me to sneeze out a whirl of glitter.

I waved the sparkles away and trudged along.

"I've searched high and low for these brown magic beans. I can't find them anywhere!" Gertie threw a dishrag over her shoulder and pushed her sleeves to her elbows. She sank her arms into a sink full of soapy water and got to work. "You'll have to rid your hangover the normal way. Scones, tea, and pumpkin juice!"

Pumpkin rolled to my ankle and wiggled his brows. I nudged him with my foot and took a seat at the table.

"No, thanks. I don't have a hangover. I'm only avoiding another round of spells. It's pointless. I've not made any progress, and each time I fade, I'm gone longer. So, why do I need to keep practicing? I think I'm going to take the day off." I shifted my gaze toward the sunlight filtering through the window.

"You need to put more heart in it, dear. That's all." Gertie sat down in front of me and pushed a plate of pastries across the table.

I grabbed the biggest scone and bit off the end, trailing crumbs down the dress I was still wearing from yesterday. "Hard to put my heart into anything when it's broken."

Gertie reached across the table and squeezed my hand. If I didn't have my fairy godmother, I would have no one. Princesses weren't born into families, and even though the other princesses in the Princess Patch were like sisters to me, I'd lost contact with most of them when Theo banished me.

"Do you still have feelings for that useless bag of bones?" Gertie asked.

"No," I sighed, finishing the pastry and licking the sticky mess off my fingers.

"Good. Because I've been in touch with other godmothers. There's this prince across the pond. His name's Prince Andrew. I never gave him much thought because he's a long way away. But—"

"Godmother! I don't want another prince. I want—" I dropped my hands to my lap and sat back in my chair.

She put her hand in the air, silencing me. "Listen, you don't have much of a choice. You have to marry a prince. There's not many available!"

"Why?"

"Because they're already married or not interested in women or—"

"No. I mean, why do I have to marry a prince?"

"Because you're a princess. It's what you do."

"I didn't ask to be born a princess. And besides, who made these rules?"

Godmother pulled the plate of pastries toward her. She grabbed a croissant and tore a chunk off with her teeth, chewing slowly.

"Well, you got me there. I have no idea who made that rule," she said between bites. "Why should you marry a prince? I've always thought you should have been taught how to take care of yourself. But then, if I can't help you with spells and getting back your princessy qualities, what is my purpose in life? To bake your breakfast every morning and charm you into clean clothes?"

She picked up her wand from the table and swished it in the air, magicking me into a new, freshly laundered dress.

"It's a start." I shrugged, smirking.

"I always knew you were different from the day I picked you. I knew you'd go far. I just didn't know how or why. I thought maybe you'd become a queen of a large regency and grow a Princess Patch of your own."

"And why couldn't I do that now? Why do I need a prince for that?" I brushed a sprinkling of crumbs from the table, letting them fall on top of Pumpkin, who nuzzled my ankle.

"Huh. You don't." She tapped her chin with her wand, jiggling her jowls.

"Exactly."

"Most princesses want the royal life. Are you sure you don't?" she asked.

"Oh no, I do. I just don't need a prince to get it." I pushed myself from the table.

Her eyes followed me to the kitchen doorway.

"I'm going to get cleaned up and head out for a walk. I don't want to talk spells or princes today. But maybe when I get back, you can tell me about this Princess Patch idea you had. And maybe you can teach me how to bake without magic. Or something without magic and without a man."

She hopped out of her chair and rushed to me, nearly stumbling over the uneven cobblestone.

"But what if you fade again while you're out there in the woods? What if you don't come back?" She wrapped her arms around me and pulled me snug into her bosom. She felt like warm pudding held together in a worn-out cheesecloth.

"I'll come back. I still have a little magic left. I made the fireplace fart earlier. Not all is lost."

"Good heavens! Go, go." She pushed me away and shooed me down the hall with her hands. "Take Trevor and Otto with you, please. The woods are dangerous!"

"I think I've met the most dangerous thing in the woods, and turns out, he's pretty friendly."

"Fake news." Grump hiccuped.

Godmother and I turned our attention to the goat who was lying on his back with all four legs in the air.

"Pardon?" I asked.

"Those vampires aren't the most dangerous things in the woods. I know. I saw it." He rolled over, stumbling to his feet but falling back down with a loud thud. His jaw opened wide as he let out a snore.

"If you come back with one more crazy enchanted—" Gertie muttered under her breath.

"I won't. Promise," I whispered, scurrying off toward my room and leaving my pitiful gang of misfits behind.

"Well, well, well. Look what the gargoyle dragged in. If it isn't Princess Pathetic. I can smell the wine on you from here. Just another typical weekday for you. I'd say those princessy qualities aren't ever going to come back. You're kind of classy but mostly not," Mirror Mirror groaned.

"Did you say I was kind of classy?" I turned around, checking my reflection in him.

He cleared his throat. "I guess I did."

"That's the first compliment you've given me since we left the castle. I'd say you haven't lost all your charm either. Maybe you aren't an asshole after all. Or maybe you're kind of charming but mostly an asshole." I blew a kiss in his direction and gave my best princess wave.

Mirror Mirror huffed out a breath, fogging his face.

By the time the haze lifted, I'd vanished into the forest.

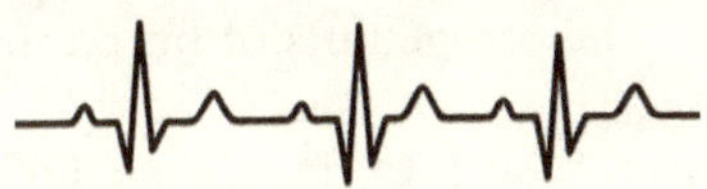

I threw on my cloak and laced my boots for my hike to the clearing I'd abandoned. I hadn't been back to my hiding spot since the day I'd met Vail. My plan to forge ahead with my royal lessons had diverted into learning to dance, donating DNA, and feeding a vampire. I only had a few short weeks to go before my debut as his fake bride at the investor ball, and by the way we'd worked the ballroom back at the winery, I'd say we were nearly ready.

I had been born to dazzle, dance, and charm. Winning over his investors would be an easy task for both of us. He complemented me, and I complemented him. Even though our audience had only been a drunken goat, we'd nailed our routine. With his grace and my bubbly personality, we were going places. Except I had no idea where I wanted to go.

I'd thought I wanted life at the court up until I was kicked out. Sure, I missed the lavish banquets. But I could have that anywhere. It wasn't until recently that I realized how much I loved going off on my own without an entourage of knights following.

I glanced beside me, patting Trevor on the head. Otto hovered above the ground, distracted by a toad. The toad jumped, startling the gargoyle and sending him crashing into a branch overhead. He zoomed off in search of the offending beast.

"What am I going to do with all of you? I've got a loyal band of friends who are about as useless as a mustache on a rat." I shook my head.

A gentle breeze rustled through the leaves as I trudged along the muddy path, crunching pine needles underfoot. Trevor paused, sniffing the air. I stuck my nose in the air and inhaled. The sweet scent of cedar and the earthy scent of moss tickled my nose. But Trevor picked up on something else. The orange tufts of fur on the back of his neck rose.

"Who're you talking to, miss?" an unfamiliar voice asked.

I turned to see a stocky, bearded man in a curious outfit. He wore a button-down jacket and pants, speckled with flecks of washed-out green and brown. Slung over his shoulder was a shotgun.

I searched the area for Otto, but he'd vanished. I'd somehow faded back into the human realm without even a dizzying warning this time.

"I was reciting poetry. Keeping my brain in shape." I tapped my finger to my temple and smiled, slowly inching backward.

Trevor let out a low growl.

"Are you lost? You don't look like you're from around here," the man said, unslinging his shotgun and pointing it at the ground.

"No. I live nearby. I came out to pick a few mushrooms for my husband. He should be coming along any minute now. He stopped a little ways back to collect a rabbit he'd killed for supper." I kept my focus on the man's weapon.

We didn't use guns much in my world, but that didn't mean we didn't have them. When our world consisted of death curses from afar and black magic to stop a criminal in his tracks, we didn't need to use human weapons.

"I see. But you're alone now. What kind of man would let a pretty thing like you roam off by yourself?" The man inched closer.

Trevor stepped in front of my legs, kicking up a pile of dead leaves. The man slowly lifted his shotgun, pointing it at my fox.

"Stop! No. He doesn't mean harm. He's protecting me."

"I've never seen someone with a pet fox. But then again, I've never seen someone dressed like you, roaming about a forest either. Where exactly did you say you came from?"

"I didn't." The sound of my heartbeat thrashed in my ears as I tried to mentally recite incantations, spells, curses—anything to bring me home.

The man tugged on his bushy beard, letting his gaze lift to mine. His eyes were as black as coal. I hadn't left the magic world. I'd only wandered into a demon.

"You're not human."

"Neither are you."

"What do you want?"

"I'm a hunter." He lifted the gun and stared down the barrel toward Trevor. "I like to play with my prey." His finger moved to the trigger. He smiled, displaying a row of sharp, jagged teeth hidden behind his lips.

I fell on top of Trevor and screamed.

A flash of black struck past me, knocking the demon off his feet. The gun fell from his hands, sliding across the forest floor and out of reach. A flock of ravens emerged in a dark cloud from overhead. They swept down into the tangle of vampire and demon wrestling on the ground.

I squeezed Trevor, who tried to escape my grasp, lunging toward the chaos. Vail gnashed his teeth, tearing chunks of flesh off the demon who didn't bleed. I stumbled backward, pulling Trevor along with me, as Vail wrestled his way atop the hunter. A howl came from behind me.

Otto hovered ahead, peeing out a bolt of lightning that zapped the demon right between the eyes, knocking him back.

"What the hell?" I whispered to my fox, who also seemed confused.

A pack of wolves leaped over us both, followed by three alligators, dozens of bats, two badgers, and a grizzly bear.

"Do it," one of the wolves howled, pacing in front of the rest of the woodland army, keeping them at bay.

Vail didn't hesitate. He clutched the demon's head between his massive hands and sank his thumbs deep into the hunter's eye sockets, mushing his evil eyes into goo.

The demon let out a bloodcurdling wail before falling limp.

Vail clenched his jaw and pushed himself off the dead body, wiping his thumbs against his pants in an inky-black streak. The beasts of the forest rushed toward the demon, tearing him apart in raw, bloodthirsty energy.

"Are you okay?" Vail squatted, putting his arms around me and lifting me to my feet.

The grunts and growls grew louder behind him.

I took one look at the carnage on the ground and the creatures fighting over it and nodded.

I reached down and ran my hand along Trevor's back, threading my fingers through his fur and giving him a comforting pat.

"He tried to kill my fox. He got what he deserved," I hissed.

Vail tilted his head, studying my face.

"Let's get you home," he said, sweeping me off my feet.

"No. It's dangerous for you. There's too much sunlight. How are you?" I scrunched my brows, craning my neck to inspect his skin. He didn't have even the tiniest bit of smolder on it.

Vail sighed, pulling me tighter against him. "About that. It turns out that you're my antidote. Which means you're the one in danger. Not me."

"But how?"

"The sunlight in your blood. Sunflower Princess. You're my sunshine," he said before pushing off his heels in a sprint toward the winery.

I swallowed hard, peeking over his shoulder to make sure my fox and guardian gargoyle were following behind us.

EIGHT

VAIL

I SLAMMED THE DOOR to the laboratory shut, leaving Penelope lying on a cot in the corner of the other room. Her pets sat atop the bed beside her, curled under her arms like baby birds under a mother's wings.

"I'm telling you, Finn, I felt it. It was a pulse," I said in a hushed voice while pacing the floor.

Finn stopped me, putting two fingers to my collar. His hand smelled of bleach.

"It's not there now! It was only one tingle a while ago. I wanted to make sure I hadn't imagined it. But today, I've been in the sunlight. And you haven't given me anything. I've only fed from her." I lifted my chin toward the laboratory windows and the princess. The bright fluorescent light ricocheted off her pale skin, giving her a moonlit glow in the middle of the day.

"And you've not had any Project X?" he asked, throwing his lab coat over his shoulders and yawning.

"No. None. I've drunk from her. That's it."

Finn brushed his palms together and smiled. His fangs stayed tucked so far up into his gums that I wouldn't have even guessed he was a vampire.

"I knew the flecks of light in her blood weren't just gold. I haven't had a chance to figure out the magic number on her blood cells and my chemical compounds to give you a dose. But now, it looks like I won't have to. Go out there and roll up your sleeves. I need to draw your blood." He reached for the doorknob.

"Wait. I need to ask something from you first. Brother to brother." I put my hand in the air, stopping him.

"Of course." He paused, resting his back against the door. "What is it?"

"Don't tell anyone. Not even Leo. Can you imagine if word got out what Penelope can do?"

"She'd be dead in a heartbeat, and, well, our hopes of a heartbeat would be gone too." Finn's voice fell flat.

"I can't let anything happen to her. She's not one of Drake's maidens or a Project X donator who knows too much. Granted, she does know too much. But still … she's more. Swear to me you won't mention this to anyone until we can figure it out together and come up with a plan?"

"You have my word. She's as precious to me as she is to you. Though for different reasons. I'm glad to see you have a sense of feeling back." He tilted his head. His messy hair swept across his brow, hiding his scar.

"What do you mean?"

"You're falling in love. She's done more than cure your allergy to the sun." He smiled, turning his back to me, and left the room.

I stood frozen, rubbing my hand over my chest and urging myself to feel something pulsing under my fingertips. But after several moments of stillness, I gave up and followed my brother out the door.

"I must have summoned them somehow. It was incredible. But you should have seen Vail! He was a monster! Ferocious! And downright scary! I never knew

Vail had that in him." Penelope motioned with her hands, clawing at the air.

"All vampires do, my lady. That's why you shouldn't trust any of them. Not even us." He held a thermometer up.

She pursed her lips as he slid it into her mouth. Her lips wrapped around it in the perfect pink O.

"Me? Ferocious? You were the one drooling at the sight of a dead demon. I knew there was something sinister lurking beneath your surface. The dismissive way you handled his death has me rethinking how innocent of a princess you are." I adjusted my pants before walking over to the cot.

Penelope narrowed her eyes and pulled the thermometer from her mouth as soon as it beeped. "I'm not! I can handle it. I just can't handle this." She glanced down as Finn sank a needle into the blue vein running through the crook of her elbow. Her head fell to the side, limp as a dishrag. Trevor and Otto both nudged it.

I sighed, smoothing her hair back and tucking a wild strand behind her ear. The clock on the wall chimed, signaling sunset.

"Did she really take it lightly? Watching you squish the window to the soul out of the demon? That's not a fun thing to watch. It's quite disgusting. Did you explain to her he wasn't gone but sent back to where he had come from?" Finn pulled the syringe out and threw it in the trash.

"I didn't explain it. I don't need her worrying. But, yeah, she took it like a champ. One threat to her furry friends, and she became much less innocent princess and much more evil queen."

"Huh. That's odd."

"Yep," I said, sticking my arm out and rolling up my sleeve. I leaned on the cot, blocking Penelope from falling.

Finn didn't bother with tying my arm. He jabbed the needle into me and took what he needed before Penelope began to stir.

"I'm going to take her upstairs to rest in my room. If you need anything else, let us know. We'll be nearby. I'll send Otto to alert her godmother that she's safe with me." I scooped her in my arms, dismissing Otto, who flew away, grumbling.

"Careful with her. She's not like your other mates." Finn peeled off his lab coat and stretched.

"You got that right," I muttered, whisking us away upstairs.

The fox followed on my heels.

Penelope woke as soon as I lowered her to my bare bed and turned on the lamp. Had I known she'd pay a visit to my sleeping quarters, I'd have prepared my lackluster room with conventional items, such as blankets and pillows. But I didn't need either. My room was nothing more than a mattress, a lamp, and a pile of dusty, old books stacked high on the nightstand. Recently, Finn had moved a cabinet full of jarred specimens to the corner of my room, claiming he'd run out of space in the laboratory. I hadn't minded. I studied those hearts nightly, looking for clues on how to make one beat again.

"What? Where am I?" She jolted upright, pressing her hands to her cheeks.

Trevor crawled on top of her lap and licked the bottom of her chin.

"You're in my room. I thought you could do with a little sleep before heading back. You've been through a lot today." I sat on the bed next to her, kicking off my shoes.

"Gertie's going to be so worried!" She scooted toward the edge of the bed, but I caught her arm and pulled her back down before she could escape.

"Otto's on it. Stay with me. Just for a little while. I want to know more about this devilish side. I'll be a gentleman." I crawled to the other end of my king-size mattress and waved. "I'll stay over here."

"Are you sure this isn't a ruse to drain me?" She dug her heels into the bed and pushed herself up to the headboard. Trevor curled beside her.

"No. It's quite the opposite actually. You're as pale as a winter's moon, and I need you alive and healthy. Your blood is my antidote. I even had a flicker of a heartbeat last we met."

"How?" She touched her hand to her collar and gasped. Her breasts swelled, nearly bursting from her laced corset.

I rubbed my eyes and rose from the bed, dragging my feet to the splintered storage cabinet. I took out a jarred heart and carried it to her.

"Is this your heart?" she asked, taking the jar and turning it in her hands.

"No, no. This is one of Finn's collectibles. Who knows who it belonged to? But this is what we're working with. You asked how I felt a heartbeat, and I don't know how to answer that. Because I thought to feel one, I'd need this." I tapped the glass.

"So, what happened to your old heart when you turned?" She handed the specimen back to me, wiping her hands down her dress.

"It turned to ash too. There's a joke between my brothers and me that ours are still there since we feel the need to revert back to life. But there's not a heartbeat to be found in the Bostwick line. At least, there wasn't."

"I'm almost too afraid to ask who all those hearts belong to then." She nodded toward the row of specimens inside the cabinet.

"Good. Don't." I turned, setting the jar back in place and shutting the cabinet.

"Tell me how it feels." She brought her knees under her chin, hugging her legs to her chest and tucking her dress under her bottom.

"How what feels?"

"The absence of a heart."

"Empty." I shrugged, lying down beside her.

"Like?"

I raised myself on one elbow. "I'm not sure how to explain it. I have the urge to feel again. Like I'm on the cusp of emotion, but I can't go over the edge. I have a hole inside of me, a void. Like heartache, I suppose."

"You know heartache?" she asked.

"Of course. I wasn't exactly innocent when I was a human. And I'm still not."

She dipped her head and pulled her legs into her tighter.

"I don't have it so bad though. Don't feel sorry for me. The only thing missing from my life is … life." I slid my finger underneath her jaw and lifted her gaze to mine. "Chin up, buttercup."

"But I can help. Maybe Finn can clone my blood and cure vampirism for good!" She perked up, clasping her hands together. "I'm good for something at least!"

"You're good for much more than a malicious beast's cure," I assured her. "Did you see the bear you summoned? And the ravens? That was all you! Magic isn't lost on you yet."

"I was reciting incantations in my head or under my breath. I have no idea how I did it." She lifted her shoulder in a half-shrug.

"Maybe your magic isn't lost. Maybe it's only changing."

"Changing? But I'm fading."

"And? Isn't that what happens to anyone who doesn't keep practicing their magic? They fade out … before disappearing completely. Use it or lose it?" I rubbed the back of my neck, ridding myself of the thought of her leaving again.

"You're saying I'm doing the wrong magic? And that's why nothing is working right? It only changed?" She chewed her lip, staring off into space. A shadow briefly fell across her face.

"I'm saying, it's a possibility." I reached over, squeezing her knee and letting my hand linger a moment too long.

"Huh." She rocked back and forth. "Interesting. I'll have to consult Gertie on this, maybe scrounge up some darker spell books and try my hand at more than a nose-hair curse."

"You should try it. Just don't curse me with anything. I've got enough on my plate," I said.

"Never! I can't have my fake fiancé with a green ogre's fungus toes twirling me around the ballroom."

"No! You can't have that. Or a case of wicked warts on the ass. That would be terrible too." I sucked a breath in through my teeth, cringing.

She slapped a hand over her mouth, stifling a giggle. A rush of pink stained her cheeks.

"Oh! Oh! I got one. How about I hex Theo with an uncomfortably heavy ballsack that rattles like Christmas bells? You can hear him jingle down the halls." She rolled on her back, laughing in deep, throaty gasps.

"Aha! A festive teste!" I pointed my finger in the air.

"Festivus testivus!" She held her hand out, as if she were holding an invisible wand, and swooshed her fingers through the air.

I cupped my balls and flinched. A sprinkling of pine needles fell from the ceiling, dusting my bed.

"You'll need to practice that one," I said while brushing off the debris.

"Definitely," she said, wiping the needles to the floor. "Hey. I meant to ask, how did you know I was there?"

"Your blood. It courses through me the same as it courses through you. When your pulse quickens, I get a tingling in my veins. I knew you were in danger when I felt a head rush. It wasn't too hard to find you. I can pick up your sunny scent from afar."

"I had no idea it worked that way. So, you're telling me you can feel when my heart races?" She squinted, studying my profile.

"I can."

"What's it doing now?" She threw her legs over the side of the bed and sat up straight, freezing in place.

"You don't have to be so still for me to read you!" I laughed. "But you're excited or nervous. It's not exactly like a heartbeat, but I can feel the thumping of your blood in my chest." I grabbed her hand and pressed her palm atop my empty rib cage. "Right here." I closed my hand over hers, stopping her trembling.

"What about now?" she whispered.

"Still thumping. Harder even."

She scooted closer to me, leaning in and burying her face in my throat. Her pulse awakened my fangs—and my dick.

"Now?" she asked, warming my neck with her soft breaths.

I locked my hands against her spine, clutching her hard against me. "Your heartbeat is deafening."

"It's because I'm not sure if I'm going to get bitten or kissed."

I pulled away, taking her hand and placing a kiss in her palm. She parted her lips and sighed.

"What would you like, Princess?" I asked.

"A little bit of both." Her mouth twisted in a grin.

I traced the soft fullness of her lip with my thumb before a sense of urgency overtook me. I crushed my lips to hers, drinking in the fiery blaze from her breath. She moaned into my mouth, hungrily returning my kiss with a reckless force. Her hand trailed down my back, tugging at my belt loops. Her pulse skittered in alarm as I ran my fingers through her hair and grabbed the back of her head, gently tilting it back and exposing her neck. My lips left hers, dragging across her cheek and down her slender neck. I kissed the pulsing hollow of her throat before sinking my fangs in deep.

"Oh," she exhaled, relaxing under my touch.

Her heartbeat slowed as I continued to suck.

"Vail!" Leo shouted, bursting through my door.

Trevor leaped from the bed, standing in front of us and growling.

I flicked my eyes upward at him before pulling away from Penelope. I swiped my arm across my lips, wiping her blood away. She left my mouth burning with fire.

"I'm so sorry. I didn't mean to interrupt. Hello, Princess." Leo bowed to Penelope before turning back toward me. "It's Drake. We have a problem at The Cave."

"On it." I rose from my bed.

Penelope rubbed her neck. I'd been as gentle as I could with her, leaving the tiniest of puncture wounds.

"Can I come too? I won't get in the way," she asked, reaching down to pat Trevor, who circled her ankles.

Leo looked at me and shrugged. "It's dangerous. But she's in your hands, not mine," he said.

"I don't think it's a place you should go, Penny. It's the underground." I pressed my lips together, but I already knew this was a battle I'd lose.

She hopped off the bed and put her hands on her hips. "Yeah, so? How do you know I haven't been there before? I've explored this cave too!"

"It's a nightclub, not a museum." I sighed.

She chewed her lip.

"Fine," I grunted. "Come on. Stick with me and don't get out of my sight. Trevor stays. There're enough animals there to keep up with already."

She bounced on her heels, jiggling her cleavage. Leo averted his eyes.

"Perfect! How are we getting there? Do you have a carriage?"

"No. We ride motorcycles." I ran my hand through my hair and took a deep breath.

"A motorcycle?" She bit her lip.

"It's like a bike with a motor," Leo explained.

"I know that! But how do I straddle that thing in this?" she asked, pointing at her ruffled dress.

"Like this." I reached down, tearing her dress in half and leaving her with a miniskirt. "You'll fit in better anyway."

Her eyes flew open. She covered her thighs with her palms, front, back, and front again. Eventually, she gave up and let her hands fall to her sides.

"Oh my Goddess! I'm nearly naked!" she shrieked.

Leo sucked in a breath, turning his back to us both. "You two are going to be trouble, and if we don't go right this instant, our entire brotherhood is on the line," he called over his shoulder.

"Yes, sir!" I saluted.

"Let's go!" Leo said, walking out the door.

Penelope took a deep breath, adjusted her smile, and followed.

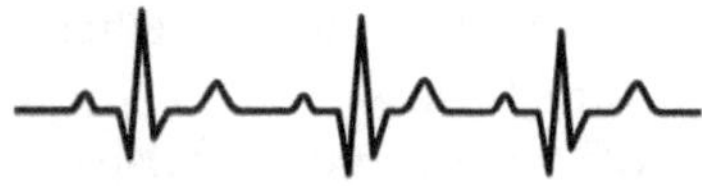

"Why didn't you ever tell me about this place?" Penelope shouted above the music echoing off the rock walls.

We'd traveled full speed on our motorcycles without issue. Penelope didn't complain once. She'd clung to me, wrapping us in an invisible warmth the entire ride. Her blood still coursed through my veins in an exhilarating pulse.

"Because the last thing you need is to hang around Morningwood's underground scene." I put my hand on the small of her back and led her inside, following Leo, Ian, and Finn.

Finn bitched and moaned about being dragged from his work, but the Bostwick brothers traveled in packs, much like the groups we'd surely come up against tonight.

"Oh, please. I like parties. Especially dance parties. Maybe I can try my hand at magicking a cake for everyone!"

She raised her hand. I caught it in mine, mid-swoop.

"No, no. None of that. We're here to fix whatever Drake screwed up, and then we're leaving."

"Speak for yourself," she muttered, blowing out a breath.

My brothers cleared the way for us, pushing aside gnomes, goblins, and fairies. A sketchy group of trolls eyed us at the entrance but stepped aside, letting us pass. Penelope wrinkled her nose. They smelled worse than Trevor on a good day.

Leo paused at the bottom of the walkway, where the cave opened up into one big room. A stage rose above the crowd in the back, where a zombie deejay spun records under flashing neon lights. Creatures big and small crowded the dance floor, whirling in lust. Whether it was bloodlust or sexual lust didn't matter, it was all the same in The Cave.

"Over there," Ian said in a long drawl, nodding to a corner table perched high up enough to see the entire club.

Priscilla sat at the table with the club owner, Bruno, along with Drake and a pack of werewolves dressed in high-fashion suits. Their eyes flashed at each small movement crossing their path.

"What's she doing here?" Penelope asked. "And who is the handsome fellow next to her? He doesn't look like a beast at all!"

I stiffened before clearing my throat and answering, "That's The Bogeyman. As in boogie man—like literally, *boogie*, like boogie down. He owns The Cave. Those two pretty much run the entire town of Morningwood."

"Like a king and queen," she sighed.

"No. Not like a king and queen. Like business partners. Neither of them involves themselves in love. It's only business for them, as is everything." I dodged a gargoyle somersaulting through the air and landing in a skid at Priscilla's feet.

"Otto!" Penelope cried.

"Come on." I grabbed her hand and dragged her through the crowd, following in the footsteps of my brothers.

A familiar eight-foot-tall night elf with skin the color of twilight stepped in front of us, blocking our path. Her hair trailed down her back, glowing like moonlight.

"Vail. Long time no see," she purred, weighing Penelope with a critical squint.

"Attalia." I bowed my head.

"Who's this?" She reached down, picking a piece of invisible dirt off of Penelope's collar and flicking it from her long, slender fingertips.

Penelope glanced at her shoulder and brushed it off.

"I'm Princess Penelope." Her smile sparkled in the dimly lit cave. "And you are?"

A howl rang out from the table up top, followed by shouting.

"Introductions later. I'm here on business. It's good to see you!" I tugged Penelope away, rushing us to Drake.

"If he can't control his bite, he'll need to leave Morningwood. It's as simple as that," Bruno said, eyeing Penelope as I set her down. He tugged his unbuttoned suit collar, exposing the enchanted gold chain hanging around his neck.

"Bruno, wait." Priscilla set her martini glass down and reached across the table, lightly touching his arm with her hand. She wore a red satin glove, reaching up to her slender elbow. Her face dazzled with a youthful radiance. She'd clearly just fed. "I need him. We can work this out. Perhaps the brothers have more news on the laboratory front. Something to curb Drake's … appetite." Priscilla looked to Finn.

"We're working on it. But you have to understand, he's new. This is our normal." Finn clasped his hands together in front of him.

Penelope gazed behind us, distracted by the thumping music and paying no attention to the danger playing out in front of her. I grabbed her hand, intertwining our fingers.

"This isn't my normal. And I don't have to put up with it." Bruno adjusted his tie. "Either control him or get out."

Drake blew out a breath and sank further into his chair.

"It won't happen again, Bruno," Leo said, directing his voice at Drake.

"All bad bitches to the dance floor!" the deejay yelled into the microphone.

The neon lights flashed in rhythm to the building beat.

"That's me," Penelope whispered. Her face split into a wide grin.

"What?" I leaned down, wondering if I'd heard her correctly over the music.

"That's me. I'm a bad bitch." She dropped my hand and hurried away, making her way to the middle of the dance floor.

Priscilla looked at me and raised her brows.

"She's going to get killed out there." Bruno licked his lips. "This is no place for a princess. Why don't you let me take her home?"

He took a fairy out of a jar and tapped her on the bottom, spreading pixie dust on the table before him. He gathered the dust in his pointed talon-like fingernail, brought it to his nose, and took a deep inhale.

"I can take care of her. Besides, she can take care of herself. We met a hunter demon in your woods today, Priscilla. Penelope summoned quite the army of ferocious beasts to deal with him. Even some of your boys were there, Bruno." I jerked my chin toward the werewolves.

"It's true. Eddie told me he felt the call and followed it. Didn't know it was her bidding," one of the wolves said with a snarl.

The other wolves howled behind him. Their attention turned toward Penelope.

She gathered what was left of her skirt in her hands and shimmied her hips on the dance floor, crushed between two elves and an ogre. One of the elves spun her, pulling her into his waist and grinding his tree limb–sized dick into her slender hips. She twerked her butt up, swaying with the music.

"I'm going to—" I growled.

Priscilla put a hand up, stopping me. "Stay here. Tell me again what you just said. She summoned wolves? And what?"

Finn jerked his eyes to me.

"I'm not exactly sure it was her. I mean, she said she thought of some spells, and all of a sudden, there were ravens and stuff." I shrugged, keeping my eyes on the elves tag-teaming my princess.

"Black magic. Bitchcraft. I thought …" Priscilla's eyes flashed. She leaned into Bruno, whispering something in his ear.

"Ah, it seems we need to borrow your princess for a minute," Bruno said, pushing up his sleeves.

"For?" I asked.

"I want to see what she can do in a threatening situation. I've got a feeling your princess might not be all princess, Vail. She might be of use after all." Priscilla brought her martini to her lips and threw back the last drops.

"What do you mean, threatening?" I shifted my weight, looking to Leo for help.

He leaned into me, muttering, "We're at their mercy. She'll be fine."

Finn drew closer to me, followed by Ian.

"So, it's okay for you to play games and get all rowdy, but I can't have a little fun?" Drake crossed his hands over his chest. His fangs gleamed in the flashing light.

"Drop it, Drake," Leo commanded, shutting up the youngest vampire.

In the middle of the cave, Penelope had drawn a circle of creatures around her. She slid this way and that, to the applause from an impressed crowd.

Priscilla smirked. "Heh. Cute. Now, throw her to the wolves." Her harsh voice cut like a knife.

"No!" I shouted.

Leo put his arm out in front of me, shoving me behind him.

"Is this really necessary?" Leo raised his voice, looking back and peering over my shoulder.

"Yes." Priscilla smiled.

The pack of werewolves leaped from the ledge and strolled toward the princess. The hairs on the backs of their heads stood on end.

Penelope threw her head back and laughed along with the dance-dueling ogre in front of her. She danced, utterly oblivious to the deadly situation creeping across the floor.

"Let me go," I sneered, jerking my shoulder from Leo.

"Easy, brother. Don't give away how important she is," Finn whispered in my ear.

Ian looked from Finn to me and back again.

He opened his mouth as if he was about to speak, but I shook my head.

"Later," I muttered.

The crowd dispersed as the wolves circled Penelope, twisting and turning. One let out a howl, followed by the rest sticking their noses in the air and growling. She looked behind her as one of the wolves rushed to her back, grabbing her from behind. The others laughed as he slid his hand across her breasts. Her blood pounded in my brain.

She squirmed out of the wolf's grasp, walking backward into the crowd. They shoved her back into the circle before stepping away and leaving her to the dogs. One werewolf started to pant, pacing in front of her. His eyes turned a putrid shade of yellow before he burst from his clothes into a hairy, muscled beast. His calves were as thick as her neck.

"Fuck this shit!" I threw my arms in the air and lunged forward.

But Bruno was beside me in an instant, holding me back. Otto whined at Priscilla's feet.

My brothers bared their fangs at him.

"Don't test me, vamps. You're on my turf," Bruno roared. His face twisted in malice.

"I won't let it go far. I want to see what she can do. You act as if you have feelings for her. But that can't be right. Vampires don't have feelings." Priscilla narrowed her eyes at me before bringing her attention back to the show at play.

Two more werewolves shifted before the first took a swipe at Penelope. His claws raked down the side of her dress, ripping it at the seams. She screamed, searching the room for help. Her forehead shone with a slick layer of sweat. My thoughts spun out of control as I struggled against Bruno and my brothers.

I let out a piercing growl, drawing her attention to me. My eyes flickered, locked on hers. I held her gaze and concentrated on the thumping of her heart.

One, two, three. One, two, three, three, I mouthed, hoping she could spin herself into a whirlwind and float away.

Her face fell flat as she repeated me, swooping her arms overhead and spinning slowly. The ground below her turned to fire. Flames licked at the ankles of the wolves, sending them off with their tails between their legs. Penelope flicked her wrist in the air and shot the largest wolf a vicious glare. A flame reached out, grabbing the wolf's ankle and dragging him to her. He struggled in painful howls, drowned out by the screaming crowd. The wolf scrambled to release himself from her fiery grasp, but it was no use. By the time he fell to Penelope's feet, he wasn't able to walk.

She rose her hand above her head and flattened her palm, sneering down at the wolf. Her lustrous locks changed from a golden sunshine hue to the empty color of midnight. She parted her lips and began to sing in a sinister tone that turned my stomach.

"Get her out of here," Priscilla shouted, rising from her seat. She threw her hands out in front of her, sending a misty haze throughout the dance floor and extinguishing the flames. "Now!" she commanded us.

Bruno dropped his arms to his sides as my brothers and I rushed toward the princess, screaming out her name. She looked to me, puzzled, before I saw the light in her eyes again. Her hair faded back to blonde.

"What was that?" Her voice trembled.

The singed wolf whined at her ankles.

"Not princessy qualities, I'm afraid," I said, picking her up and slinging her over my shoulder. She blazed like the sun against my skin.

NINE

PENELOPE

I ROLLED OVER IN bed and yawned.

By the time I'd made it back to my cottage, it was well past midnight. Gertie had stayed up all evening, waiting on my arrival but didn't pressure me to talk once I made it home. Instead, she shook her wand in Vail's face and questioned him while I nodded off, nearly stumbling to the floor. Whatever magic I'd performed drained me.

"The devil arises!" Mirror Mirror said.

Trevor stretched his paws out in front of him, arching his back. Otto tried to mimic the clever fox, but he fell off the bed, smacking his smooshed face on the stone floor.

"I give it a two out of ten," Grump said. "You need to work on your dismount, bat boy."

Otto stuck his tongue out at the goat.

"Can I not live a normal life?" I rubbed my eyes and pushed myself up on my elbows, peering into Mirror Mirror.

The woman staring back at me looked as if she'd been buried, dug up again, buried once more, and then risen from the grave. My bloodshot eyes looked out over dark circles framing my sunken-in sockets. The hair on my head was knotted in bird's-nest tangles. My skin glowed a ghostly shade, almost fluorescent. The rosy flush that normally graced my cheeks had vanished.

I plopped back down on the bed and pulled the blanket over my head.

"I'd do that, too, if I looked like a walking troll turd," Mirror Mirror muttered.

"Rise and shine, Penelope. You've got some explaining to do," Gertie said, barging in my room.

"She isn't rising or shining. She's only decaying," Mirror Mirror said.

"Well, she can decay all she wants." Gertie snatched the blanket from the bed, exposing my lifeless form. "But on her time."

"What do I need to do? Can't I just rest? I had a long night," I groaned.

"That you did. And you'll never do that again to me, missy! An old lady like me could drop dead of a heart attack, waiting around on you all day and night. First, it was the vamps, then it was a demon, and now the wolves! You're meddling with the wrong crowd. I had a bad feeling about this, and now, it's all coming together. What next? Are you thinking of bringing home a leprechaun?" She balled the blanket up in her arms and stood frozen, waiting on a response.

"Will he bring me enough gold to get out of this shithole?" I asked, throwing my arms in the air.

"No! That's your job. And instead of practicing your princessy qualities, you're going to nightclubs, fighting werewolves, letting a vampire suck on you."

I jerked my eyes to hers.

"Yes, yes. I saw that bite mark on your neck! Can't fool me." She pressed her lips into a thin line and turned on her heels, disappearing into the kitchen.

I threw my legs over the edge of the bed and stretched. Pumpkin rolled into the room and situated himself between my feet, waiting on me to rise so he could catch a glimpse under my gown. He'd performed that trick numerous times before I finally caught on to it. Trevor hopped off the bed and swished his tail at the garden vegetable, sending him flying under the bed. The smell of fresh-baked scones and hot tea drifted down the hall, slowly waking me. I rose to my feet and shuffled past Godmother and toward the kitchen.

A fading, evening sunlight filtered through the window, past the drying herbs she'd hung from the rafters. The scent of clover, lavender, and a peppery herb I couldn't identify tickled my nose.

"You're practicing herbs and medicines again?" I asked.

I pulled out a chair and made myself comfortable at the table. Sugar scattered across the tabletop, where Gertie sat, mumbling into her teacup. Two wet teabags were perched on a spoon next to her.

"You never know when you might need a poultice. Winter will be here soon. I don't want any sneezy snots or coughing clots in the house. We need to keep ourselves healthy." She poured a steaming stream of tea from the kettle into a chipped mug before pushing the cup toward me. "Take this."

I sniffed the cup and flinched. "What is this? It smells worse than Trevor!"

I pushed the cup back to her, but she shook her head and gave it back.

"Ox broth with a few other strengthening herbs. Vail mentioned you had a long day and night and needed all the rest you could get. You slept the entire day." She glanced out the window.

I held my breath and threw the cup of tea back, swallowing the entire cup in three gulps. I reached for the plate of scones and tore into one, ridding the bitter taste of ox from my mouth before I could speak again. "Did he tell you anything else? Besides that we were attacked by a demon and wolves. Or did he tell you about my labs?"

"He told me you'd explain it because he wasn't quite sure what was going on either. He had to rush home and prep for the ball."

"The ball." My voice fell flat. "Crap. That's this weekend. I've been so busy that I haven't even given Theo a second thought!"

"Busy with wolves. Tell me about last night." She folded her arms and rested them on the table.

"It started yesterday when I came across the demon in the woods. I think I did black magic. I repeated something in my head, and I summoned ravens and a bear even! And the wolves!"

She took a deep breath.

"And then last night, at The Cave ... well, it all happened so fast. I'm not entirely sure how it went down, but I think I felt threatened and scared, and the next thing I knew, I did a twirl and set the place on fire, singeing a few werewolves." I bit into another scone, smacking my lips.

She buried her head in her hands and rubbed her temples. "That's dark magic. Maybe even mixed with bitchcraft. How did you know how to do those spells?"

"I'm not sure. But Vail said maybe my magic isn't fading. It's changing. And if I practice the magic I'm supposed to be doing, then maybe I'll stop fading too." I pushed myself from the table and walked to the cupboard, filling a glass of water before sitting back down.

"But why?" She looked up at me. "Why's it changing? What made it change, and how can we stop it and bring the old princess back?"

"I don't know. But ... I kind of like it. Not the maniac part, but I like being able to do more than sprout a flower from my steps or cause a shower of rainbow sprinkles for a birthday party. I think maybe I can do some good with this." I brought the glass of water to my lips and chugged it down.

"Good? With black magic?"

"Maybe. I don't know how, but I'll figure it out. I just need to practice some darker spells. But first, I have to meet Vail again tonight. Last practice before showtime." I rubbed my neck, where he'd left his mark. My inner thighs flushed.

I'd kissed my fair share of princes and frogs, but I'd never kissed a vampire. After the silken touch of Vail's lips on mine, I knew whatever fake relationship we had was a lie to ourselves along with everyone else. There was something there between us, and it wasn't my dark arts and life-giving blood. Vail and I could become powerful together.

"There's something else." I braced myself against the back of the chair. The straw backing poked through my gown and itched my back.

"Oh no. What?" she asked.

"I'm the cure."

"For?"

"Vampirism."

She slumped in her chair, dropping her mouth in a trembling pout.

"Then, you're not safe." She lifted her misty eyes to mine.

"I'll be fine. I can throw a fireball or something at anyone who gets in my way!" I reached across the table, covering her hand with mine.

"Everyone will come looking for you if word of this gets out. There'll be a lot of vampires who will want you dead. We must leave soon." She pushed herself from the table and brought the teapot to the sink, emptying it.

"I can't leave! I have the investor ball. I want to see the look on Theo's face when he recognizes me. Remember? That's been the plan all along!" I wrung my hands, swallowing the lump forming in my throat.

"I'll give you that and only that. You're still in my care, and I'm telling you, we're leaving after the ball." She turned back toward me.

"But where do we go?"

"I don't know. It's just not safe in Morningwood anymore. I'm going to do some research and try to understand what's going on with your magic. Maybe I'll find some not-so-harmful stuff you can practice. I guess the good thing about you performing magic means you won't fade away anymore—if you practice it right," she said.

I thought back to Fritzi and the magic bean water and how she'd shown me all sorts of curiosities in the diner and outside in her world. I wished I could help her to come back and experience all she'd missed on her brief visit to the fantastical. But the magic realm was my home. And no human was worth me giving that up—not even my new friend.

"Yeah, yeah. I know. If I don't use it, I lose it. I don't want to go back there anyway." I stood up and stretched my arms over my head, nearly knocking down a bundle of lavender.

"Right." She dragged her slippers across the floor, stopping in front of me. The corner of her mouth turned up in a smile that wasn't genuine, revealed by her trembling lips.

"Godmother, will you at least come to the ball and see my debut? Since we have to disappear after. It'll probably be a long time before we can celebrate again. It'll be like old times. We can dance and drink champagne, and they'll have cake!"

"I wouldn't miss it for the world." She pulled me into a tight embrace, sinking me into the doughy folds of her bosom. Her heart raced, thumping hard against my cheek.

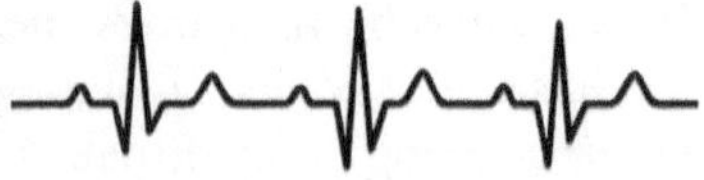

At my godmother's insistence, I took the car to the winery and skipped my usual walk. She'd sent me along with Trevor, Otto, Grump, and what she called a can of whoop-ass. All I had to do was pop the top on it, and a rain of fists would pummel my opponent, knocking him out while I made my getaway.

I'd never seen such a thing before, but with Gertie's habit of collecting oddities, I wasn't surprised by her new gift. Once, she'd brought home a charmed record player that played songs according to the owner's mood. But after it sang out a rendition of kinky, sexy music during a dinner party, Gertie sent him straight to the trash bin. I'd always known she had a thing for Marti, the magician.

I drove the car down the gravel drive, past rows of yellowing, leafy vines tethered to wire and posts. The full moon lit the entire field, giving me an impressive view of a place I'd never paid much attention to. I pulled my car around the back of the fortress-like winery, swerving around a line of topiaries decorating the front path. Vail's home was beautiful, but it needed a woman's touch. The chill in the air surrounding his place was less than welcoming.

Otto bounced in his seat, shaking the can of whoop-ass.

"Put that down!" I cried a moment too late.

A giant's hairy fist burst forth, smashing Grump straight between his eyes. The goat screamed before falling over into the backseat.

"Damn it! That's why I told you all to stay put. No touching anything! You should have listened, Otto!"

The gargoyle shrank in his seat in a lipless pout.

Trevor flicked his tail in the air and looked away.

I slammed the car to a stop, parking it in front of the ballroom. I hopped out, opening the back door and cursing to myself.

"Problem?" a voice called behind me.

I turned to see Drake, fangs out, watching me bend over the backseat. He pushed his hair from his eyes.

"My goat. He's knocked out." I tugged Grump's hooves, wrestling him out of the car. The goat wouldn't budge.

"Allow me," Drake said. He nudged me aside, swiftly picking up Grump and laying him on the grass. He scrunched his nose. "He smells like wine mixed with horse shit."

"He's a drunk … and a goat." I gave him a dismissive wave.

His eyes lingered on me longer than I felt comfortable with. I leaned down, stroking Grump's neck to try to wake him.

"There you are!" Vail rushed to my side, eyeing the goat. "Oh no! Did you run over him?"

"No! Of course not! This was Otto opening a can of whoop-ass!"

Drake clutched his sides and laughed, exposing his fangs.

Grump stirred, rolling his head from side to side. The tufts of hair on his chin trembled.

"I give it a ten out of ten," he heaved, his voice harsh and breathless.

"Never knew I'd be rescuing drunk goats and evil princesses when I asked to be turned." Drake shook his head. "Now, if you'll excuse me, I'm running late. Priscilla has a lead on virgin twins who she wants me to charm. She said if I'm successful, I can keep one to play with." He smirked, licking the tips of his fangs before running away.

The dirt from the gravel drive kicked up in his wake.

"Does he seduce them to their death?" I swallowed hard.

"Best you not know about that business arrangement." Vail scooped Grump in his arms. "Come on. Let's get this rotten farm animal to the ballroom, so coyotes don't use him as a snack. Wait until you see it in there! It's going to be a spectacular event!"

I motioned for my pets to follow as we made our way through the giant arched doorway and into the grandest venue I'd ever seen. The Bostwick wine label was painted in glossy black across the wooden dance floor. Tables covered in white cloth circled the logo, leaving enough room for dancing and mingling. Overhead, a warm glow came from a handful of stage lights lining the sides of where the chandelier would hang.

Vail squatted, lowering the sleepy goat to the floor.

"Go on. Check it out," he said, tilting his head toward the lavishly decorated tables.

A wide smile played across my face as I skipped toward a table, admiring the bouquet centerpieces. Vail clasped his hands behind his back and followed me, grinning from ear to ear. I plucked a sunflower from a crystal vase, brought it to my nose, and took a deep breath.

"It smells like you, doesn't it?" he said, placing his palm on the small of my back.

My skin prickled under his touch.

"It smells like home," I breathed out before placing the flower back in its vase.

"They're from Lily's Flower Emporium. I paid extra to have her enchant them. They'll never wilt."

I dragged my hand across the white tablecloth, touching the sunflower-etched fine china and the golden napkin rings holding a miniature sunflower tucked into the cloth napkins.

"This is beautiful," I whispered, wiping my eyes.

"Anything for my bride." He loomed closer, leaving no room between us.

I bowed my head and sniffled.

"Hey, look"—his fingers clamped my trembling chin, lifting it and forcing my gaze on his—"I know what happened to you at your wedding really damaged you. So, I wanted to do this for you. Maybe give you something like the wedding you didn't get. Take this as your party. Take it as a new beginning. You've already come so far from the innocent princess I found singing birdsongs in the forest."

I stepped back, taking a deep and unsteady breath. "Why? Why would you do this for me?"

"Because you're quite literally my sunshine." He wrapped his hands around my hips, digging his fingertips into my soft flesh and pulling me into him. His cock stiffened against my thigh like a cold rod of steel.

"Take me to bed. I want to feel you pulse inside of me while I pulse inside of you." I reached up, cupping his jaw in my palm. My breasts strained against my tight blouse with each ragged breath I took.

His dark eyes grew wild, dropping from my gaze to my shoulders to my breasts. A hint of fang peeked out from under his lips.

"Right this way, Your Majesty," he said, sweeping me off my feet like I was weightless.

My heartbeat skyrocketed.

He carried me to his bedroom and put me back on my feet before I could give my decision a second thought.

"You're sure?" he asked, towering over me.

"I can't have vampire babies, right? And you're immune to stuff? Or is there a vampire pox I don't know about?" My breath caught in my throat as I nudged him toward the wall.

"You're safe with me. Always." His voice deepened in a rough growl.

He swallowed hard as I dropped to my knees.

I ran my palm up his thigh, feeling his erection under his pants. A flicker of excitement coursed through my veins as I pulled him out entirely and wrapped both of my hands around his thickness. I touched my lips to the tip of his cock and lazily swirled my tongue under the head. My eyes snapped up, locking on his, while I took my time playing. I lay my palms flat against his hips, pressing him hard into the wall behind him and holding back his thrusts.

His lids slipped over his eyes as he buried his hands in my hair and pushed my mouth toward him. He lifted his hips, holding my head steady in his hands. His cock slid over my tongue and down the back of my throat, gagging me in a newfound pleasure. A moan escaped his lips when I struggled to pull back. He let go, letting me catch my breath for a quick moment before crushing his cock into my skull again. I reached down, beneath my skirt, and rubbed my fingertips across my clit.

He roughly pulled me to my feet, holding my waist in an iron grip. I wiped the back of my hand across my wet mouth and caught my breath.

"Your innocence is merely a smoke screen, Princess." He flicked open the buttons on my blouse, one by one, letting it fall to the floor.

"That's because you set me on fire," I said, shimmying out of my skirt with urgency.

He tore off his clothes and grunted, tossing me onto the bed and easing my knees apart. The lean muscles of his abs scraped against my soft belly as he crawled on top and kissed me. His erection brushed against my inner thigh. The touch of his lips sent a shock wave down my body, settling between my legs. His fangs brushed against my skin as he worked his way from my lips to my breasts. He flicked his tongue over each of my firm nipples before taking one in his mouth and sucking.

I bit my lip, stifling a moan as he worked his way down. He teased my pussy lips apart with the cool brush of his fingertips before sliding a finger deep into me. He worked his finger in and out. I arched my hips, aching for him to taste me when I finally felt his mouth on me. The cold flame of his tongue licked me from top to bottom in short, feathery strokes. I bucked my hips and grasped his shoulders, tugging him back up.

He rose above me, rubbing his dick between my pussy lips. He paused at my entrance, bared his fangs, and sank his mouth and cock deep into me. My blood hummed in my veins as he sucked the crook of my neck while burying himself into me in an explosive rush. I slipped upward, rubbing my clit against him with each thrust.

Tingles ricocheted off me as my legs began to tremble. I cried out for release when he pulled himself up, rising above me with a wicked stare. He picked up his rhythm and moved his hand to my neck, clasping around the spot he'd bitten. My breaths stopped, but the waves of pleasure washing over me pulsed in spastic ripples. I bucked against him in a freeing burst of fire. He threw back his head and moaned, giving me one last final push before I felt him spill out inside of me.

His flesh fused with mine as he collapsed, gently pressing his lips to my wound in soft pecks. His once-icy lips scorched my skin.

"Why haven't I been having sex with vampires all this time?" I said out loud in a dumb post-sex stupor.

He rolled off of me and burst out in laughter. I joined in, still giggly from my orgasm.

"Oops. I didn't mean to say that out loud. I'm not the promiscuous type of princess or anything. Believe me, there are those. But I'm innocent. I just—" I sucked in a breath.

"Shh. Come here." He grinned, putting his arm under my shoulders and pulling me close.

I nestled in next to him and rested my head against his chest.

I felt a slight pulse under my cheek.

"I feel it!" I shouted, bolting upright.

"I did too. But it doesn't last long." He rubbed his hand across his chest. "I didn't feed much on you. I wanted my vampire wit about me for the event this weekend. But still, let's enjoy this. Lie with me." He reached out, tugging me back down to him.

I lay my head back on him and listened as his body vibrated with new life.

For the rest of the week, I forgot about practicing spells, and instead, I lost myself in raw passion.

TEN

VAIL

I LAY IN BED, staring at the ceiling and pondering my task list for tomorrow's event. Penelope's sugary scent lingered in my new silken bedsheets.

I'd picked them up after the first time I took her to bed. The next day, when she came for her "lesson," I proudly showcased the gold-trimmed linens tucked under a massive pile of feathered pillows. She took one look at our nest and leaped onto the bed, tossing herself on her back and begging for me. I hadn't hesitated to come when she called. She might not have been able to summon the sweet friends she used to, but she could easily summon me. One flutter of the princess's full lashes, and my fangs dropped.

After our last meeting, she'd asked me what it was like to turn and feel life slip away. I explained to her my poison's properties, such as gnawing dread, restless anxiety, and the dull, numbing pain that carried my prey to death. These feelings would overtake the victim at high doses, leaving him in a horrifying mental state until the light left his eyes.

But in lower doses, my poison was torture, causing the victim to suffer, knowing death was at his door. His heart would burn inside of his chest, searing him with blinding pain until he begged for me to end him and turn it all to ash. There was no easy way to inject poison and end life—for feeding or otherwise.

A rolling knock thumped against my door.

"Yes?" I asked.

"It's Finn. I need to talk to you." His voice was distant and hurried.

"Come in."

I pushed myself up on my elbows and sighed. I'd avoided Finn all week, reluctant to share Penny and her miraculous blood. It wasn't exactly a secret that she'd been in my bed for days. My brothers teased me in the rare moments they found me alone. But true to his word, Finn never mentioned the new developments with her DNA to anyone. Otherwise, Leo would have already stopped our sexcapades and had the princess under strict lockdown.

"Jeez. How much blood have you been drinking? You're practically blushing!" Finn whispered, closing the door behind him.

"Barely any! I don't want to be human for the event. I'm supposed to be on my toes, and, well, human me was much less quick and agile when I danced. I think I stepped on a foot here and there. But vampire Vail can twirl Penelope in the air like she's weightless. So, I figured I'd better hold back."

"Doesn't look like you're holding back anything," he said, plopping down beside me and adjusting the pillows under him.

"I mean, I'm only holding back the bloodsucking. All else is free game." I rubbed the scruff along my jawline.

"I need to get out more," Finn moaned, threading a hand through his hair. "But work."

"Which is why you're here." I raised my brows.

"Yep. I injected myself with a very, very tiny portion of her blood to see if her DNA would work with all vampires."

"And?"

He brought his fingertips to his cheeks. "And I was able to feel the sun on my face without peeling away." A wide grin spread across his face.

I shifted my weight and rose to a sitting position. "Okay. What does this mean for her?"

"It means, we have to tell Leo first. He will know what exactly we need to do to keep her under wraps. Secondly, we need far more testing. Once we get the green light from him, I'll start injecting you with her blood. You can't drink it from her. I need to make sure our compound works. We'll go through some trials. If it's a success for a few hours of sunlight, we'll push further with a control group. But that's the tricky part. How do we recruit a control group without sounding the alarm to those Council bastards?"

"Vail?" Leo's voice called from the other side of the door.

"Shit." I stood up, running my palms down my thighs.

"Are you sweating?" Finn asked.

"It's just a slightly damp film across my hand. It comes and goes."

Finn tapped his chin before pulling a notepad and pen from his front pocket and scribbling in it.

"Vail, are you in there?" Leo shouted through the door.

"Come in!" I answered.

Leo nudged open the door.

"I was coming to talk business, but it looks like you're way ahead of me. By the looks on your faces, I'm not sure why I wasn't asked to attend this serious meeting." He stood in the doorway, leaning against the frame. His deep-set eyes narrowed below gray-flecked brows.

Finn looked from Leo to me and back again.

"We were just about to find you and give you some news. Would you like to sit down?" I held my hand out toward the bed and added chairs to my mental shopping list.

"I'll stand. Is this about the investors? Our bank account is dwindling, and no one has updated me on the status of the investor ball." His voice was firm and edged with a particular caution that could only be learned from years on the battlefield. Leo folded his arms across his broad chest, nearly bursting out of his army-green button-down.

"No, it's not that. I've all of that under control. I promise." Dipping my head, I said, "Finn, you know more than I do about the labs. Can you explain? I'll fill in the details about Penelope."

"Ah, right. Okay. It seems we've had a bit of a breakthrough in our research. Penelope's DNA is proving to be quite useful." Finn chewed the end of his pen.

Leo straightened his back, letting his arms fall to his sides. "Useful how?"

"We've run minimal tests, but both Vail and I were able to withstand the sun for short periods—very short periods. I don't know exactly how long the effect will hold out or if it will cure us completely until we run more trials, which means, I'll need more trustworthy vampires who want to revert to their human form."

"She's the cure?" Leo looked at me.

Finn cleared his throat. "She's a *possible* cure."

"And what sets her apart from everything else we've tested?" Leo lowered his voice and shut the door behind him.

"We've never tested a princess before. It could be all princesses who share this ability, or it could be just her—born of the sunflower."

"And how rare is that?" Leo asked.

"She's the only one alive." Finn's voice fell flat.

I snapped my eyes to his. "How do you know this?"

"I've done some digging. There are only three working Princess Patches in the world. The sunflower only grows in the southernmost patch. The last one to bear a child was Penelope's. There's promising research that says the patch might experience another sunflower bloom this summer, but as of now, Penelope is the only sunflower princess."

A sheen of slick heat prickled at the base of my hairline.

"Get her in here and get more of her DNA. I want jugs of it." Leo's tone became chilly.

"Wait! We can't put her through anything painful or harsh or drain her! She's not a vampire. We don't believe in harming others if it's not needed, remember? We're different." My voice shook.

Leo took two strides toward me and grabbed my shoulders, squeezing them under a harsh grip. "I remember the cause. I remember why we started this laboratory in the first place. It's not for love. It's for life. Of course we won't drain her. We need her. But we need to start testing before word gets out and it's too late. She just became our biggest asset and The Council's biggest enemy," Leo said, pushing away from me.

A rush of emotions raged within me. I thought back to the day I'd met Penelope, twirling, mid-birdsong, in the middle of the forest. Her perpetual merriment had been contagious, softening me in ways her blood couldn't.

"Can I have your word that she's protected? We won't put her through any unnecessary torture?" I searched his eyes but only found the usual void that signaled he had been dead for far too long.

"Brother, I see the gleam sparkling within you even now, and I'm happy for you. I want both of you to feel it and Ian too. Drake, if he wants it." Leo sighed. "And, yes, I also want new life to beat in my chest, so when I have a true death, I can leave this world peacefully among my soldiers. But I'm in my own personal battlefield, and your princess carries my winning flag. I'll not let anything harm her. You have my word. But do not cross me in this war—for sex, for feelings, or for love. I won't surrender."

"Understood," I muttered.

"Good. Keep me up-to-date with the latest reports. I want them daily. Twice daily actually," Leo said, turning on his heels and marching out of my room.

Finn rose to his feet and patted my back on the way out the door. "Don't worry. I'm already toying with cloning her. If we can figure out how to grow more blooming sunflowers that hatch royal blood, Penelope will no longer be of use. You two can run away and *live* your lives."

I could only manage a faint nod of my head while I stared after him in speechless confusion.

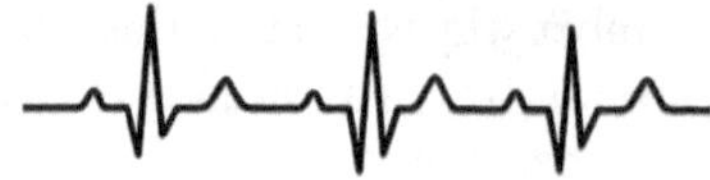

I spent the rest of the day in the laboratory with Penelope, feeding her wine and cheese and spoiling her while Finn poked and prodded her fragile body. My puncture wounds had all but disappeared from her slender white neck. I'd refused to drink from her the last two times we made love despite her softening shoulders beckoning me to nuzzle my mouth in the dip of her collar.

I watched her animated expression as she lay back on the cot, discussing our new change in the dance routine with Finn. She opened her full red mouth and let out a loud laugh along with Grump as they argued over which part of the performance was the best.

"So, what you're saying is, I can't miss it." Finn tossed a cotton ball in the trash and wheeled his stool back beside Penny. He loosened the tourniquet on her arm, thumping her veins.

"You won't want to. Besides, I was going to ask if you'd introduce us. You know how that asshole Theo will be there. I need someone who can convince the crowd that our love is real." My voice trailed off as I realized what I'd said out loud. "Not that I don't love you. I mean … someday, I—"

"Oh, hush." She playfully smacked my forearm with the light touch of her fingertips. "If you had told me you loved me after the first week we'd been making magic, I would have run for the hills! Red flags and all."

"You'd have promptly fallen into his arms and declared yourself his. You'd already be planning your Princess Patch with him right this second." Grump stuck his head in a bowl of wine and took a gulp.

"You got me there." She hiccuped. "Bad decisions is my middle name."

"Hold still, Penelope Bad Decisions. You're going to feel a slight prick." Finn guided the needle into the crook of her arm, but Penelope had already passed out.

"What did you mean by planning a Princess Patch, Grump? How does one do that exactly?" I asked.

"Why? You want babies?" The scraggly goat's beard shook beneath whiskered lips. "To eat?" He let out a scream.

"No! We don't eat babies! I didn't know Penny wanted babies. Princess Patches are rare. I've known kings and queens who have tried growing them for years."

Penelope's color drained from her face with each vial Finn took.

"They're rare all right, and the rarest specimen I've ever been able to test is sitting right here, fast asleep." Finn pulled the syringe from her arm, pressing a bandage directly on her wound. Her golden-flecked blood swirled, sparkling in the glass tubes.

"Knowing her, she's pretending to be asleep and waiting for you to kiss her, so she can wake and claim it was true love's kiss." Grump chewed a side of the bedsheet hanging from the corner of the cot.

I smirked, bending over and placing a kiss on Penelope's lips. She tasted like Black Label.

The goat tilted his head.

Penelope had a quick intake of breath, followed by little short gasps.

"I don't feel so well," she moaned.

"I give your love a ten out of ten." Grump stuck his head back in his wine bucket.

"I'll get you some water." Finn patted the top of her head.

"I'm not that sick. I'll take more wine." She gave him a dismissive wave.

"She lives." I smiled, placing another kiss on her lips.

"You two were made for each other. Let's figure out how to get you two together without the whole immortality versus mortality thing hanging over your head," Finn whispered in my ear before disappearing from the room.

"How romantic." My smile faded as I pushed the thought from my mind.

I filled her wineglass and handed it to her, placing it in her weak grip. Her fingers shook as they wrapped around the stem.

"Allow me," I said, taking the glass back and putting it to her lips.

She took a long sip and smiled with cranberry-stained teeth. For a moment, I had a flash of what she'd look like if she were a vampire—dabbing the blood off of the corners of her mouth with a white linen napkin.

"I'm still weak. Guess I'll not be able to practice the dance. Maybe you should take me to your bedroom to lie down." She pushed herself up, threw her legs over the side of the cot, and wobbled into my arms. Her hair flowed like honey down her back, tangling in my hands.

"As tempting as that is, I think I'd better get you home. You need rest after all of this testing if you're going to be at your best tomorrow. It's your big day!" I dipped her, tracing my finger down the crown of her head, over the tip of her nose, and pausing at her pout. Her lips parted at my touch.

"And then?" she asked as I stood her back upright.

"And then you can live your life anew. Start fresh and find a new goal. Hopefully, a much healthier one than revenge. Maybe open a bakery or a tea shop."

"Hmm," she said, gazing upward at the ceiling. "I'm not much of a baker or a tea connoisseur. Perhaps Godmother can help me think of something. I can't exactly sit around, singing birdsongs all day and expecting squirrels to clean my kitchen. She mentioned trying to find out what went wrong back at The Cave, so we can work on whatever is happening to me. If I'm a demon witch, maybe I can conjure Karma potions or send an army of rats to swarm Troll City next time they threaten an invasion."

"Easy, tiger. It's all about what you want—and only what *you* want. If summoning beasts to assault assholes makes you happy, then we'll find a way to do it."

"We?"

"I'm not going anywhere. Are you trying to get rid of me after this affair?" I brushed the pad of my thumb down her cheek, cupping her jaw in my palm.

"No. But there's something I need to tell you." She swayed, nearly knocking into Grump, who was passed out on the floor behind her.

Finn barged back into the room with his lab coat flying behind him. "All set. I think I'm good for now. We can do another round after the ball. Now, I've got a lot of work to do, and I need zero interruptions. You're dismissed!" He threw his hands in the air, shooing us away.

I glanced at the goat, too distracted to fool with him.

"Can you send Grump home when he wakes?" I asked, following Penny out the door.

"I'll have Drake run him over shortly. Have fun, you two fake lovebirds. I can't wait to lie through my fangs to the crowd tomorrow on your behalf."

"On yours too! You'll likely have enough to buy some new equipment after all of the investors are dazzled." I took Penelope's hand, twirling her in an embrace.

"*Ta-da*!" she sang.

"As I said, you were meant for each other." He shook his head and returned to work.

"Ahem." I cleared my throat as we made our way out of the laboratory and toward the exit. "You were saying?"

Penelope paused, turning toward me. The animation had left her face. "I have to go after tomorrow."

"Go where?"

"I don't know. Godmother said it's not safe for me here. I gave all I could today. You all damn near drained me. I can try to get more blood to you here and there. But when my fairy godmother is worried, there's usually a good reason." She reached out, placing her hand over my arm. "Is there a good reason?"

I hung my head. My mind whirled with how to keep her safe yet close while hiding her from everyone—including my brothers. If Leo knew she was leaving, he'd have her locked in the basement.

I glanced down the hall behind me before lowering my voice. "There is. Let me speak with your godmother after the dance, and perhaps I can help you escape." I shifted my weight from one foot to the other.

"But I don't want to go," she pleaded in a barely audible whisper.

"Remember what I said about starting anew? Best to do that somewhere new too. Princess Penelope's Tea and Dark Arts, or Pie and Die, or Murder by Muffins, or Penny's Brown Magic Bean Water."

The corner of her lip turned up in a halfhearted grin. But the smile on her face faded as quickly as it had come.

"I'll see what I can do." Her voice grew unsteady. "This place was finally growing on me. My crumbling cottage and army of royal misfits. Everything." Her shoulders slumped. "Even you."

I held out my arms, motioning for her to lay her head on my empty rib cage.

"You've grown on me too, Your Majesty. You've been a ray of sunshine in my eternal dusk." I kissed the top of her head, breathing her in for what I knew would be one of the last times.

ELEVEN

PENELOPE

I STUCK MY TOE inside the bathtub faucet, letting the warm water wash over my silky, smooth legs. An anxious feeling arose in my stomach, catching in my throat every time I thought about Theo. In a few short hours, he would arrive at my vampire lover's lair, and I would finally get to show him what he'd lost. Despite my lack of magical skills these days, I had other princessy qualities. I ran a house full of enchanted pets, my heart was as big as my alcohol tolerance, and I'd charmed my way into a brotherhood of villains, helping them with a good cause. I was practically my own charity.

I swirled my hands beneath the warm water, scooping up a handful of bubbles and blowing them to Trevor and Otto, who lay on the rug beside me. The ashen skin on Otto's rounded, full belly pulled taut, stretching out like he'd swallowed Pumpkin. By the loose feathers stuck in Trevor's hair, I had an idea the duo had guzzled an entire chicken coop for dinner.

"Knock, knock!" Godmother called in a singsong voice.

"Come in." I adjusted the bubbles over my naked body.

"What do you think? Too much?" Gertie stepped into the candlelit bathroom and twirled. Her silken purple robes flowed out beneath her like a blooming flower. Her gray hair lay twisted on top of her head in an updo so tight that her skin pulled, making her look ten years younger.

"You look gorgeous!" I said, nearly sliding under the water.

"Like old times, isn't it?" She beamed. "I haven't done anything like this in ages."

"It's been less than a year!"

"It's been one rough year," she said.

Otto stuck out a finger and poked her snakeskin slippers. The clasp on the top hissed, scaring him out the door. Trevor lifted his head for a moment but laid it back down with a loud breath.

"But after tonight, we start fresh," I said, avoiding her gaze.

"I know you don't want to, and I don't either. But I can't have my goddaughter in a dangerous situation like this. It's beyond anything I can protect you against. Besides, we still don't know what you're capable of. That could make things worse." She walked to the mirror above the sink and wiped the fog away before giving her reflection a look of satisfaction. "You haven't even cracked one of those spell books I brought back for you, have you?" She turned back toward me.

"I've not had the chance. I've been practicing my routine." I dipped my head under the water and back up again, wiping away the perfumed bubbles clinging to my face.

"You can't hide from me. I saw the bite marks on your neck, and by how much time you've been spending with Vail, I'm assuming that's not the only place they are."

"Doesn't matter anymore. Not if I'm running away tomorrow."

"No. I guess it doesn't. So, let's make tonight amazing. We'll dazzle that old jackass Theo, and you can party with your vampire lover until the wee hours of the night. But at dawn, we vanish." Her voice fell into a whisper.

I sniffled and reached for a towel to dry my face.

Otto peered around the doorway before waddling back into the room. He plopped down next to Trevor, covering himself with the fox's tail. Trevor peeked from beneath his lashes and fell back asleep. Gertie sighed and left the room, shutting the door behind her.

I hummed an old lullaby that usually sent snowflakes whirling through the air, instantly lifting my mood. But nothing happened, except the bubbles in my bath popping simultaneously in a string of ridiculously loud farts.

"I give it a ten out of ten!" Grump called from the other room.

"Classy!" Mirror Mirror echoed.

I pushed myself out of the water and cringed. Perhaps it was best I left Morningwood and my failures behind.

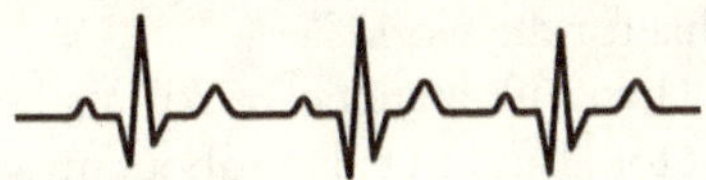

We entered the ballroom through the back door. Gertie had insisted our pets stay home and out of the way, so we wouldn't make a spectacle of ourselves. I'd flinched, watching Otto fumble his finger up his nose, and agreed. The last thing I needed was for Theo to think he'd made the right decision. All of my hard work from the year hinged on tonight's plan executing perfectly.

Gertie hung our cloaks as I gathered my skirt in my fists and marched across the ballroom toward the man who had helped me make my dream come true. Vail stood, towering over the gnomish waitstaff setting up the catering tables. His inky-black eyes matched his well-tailored tuxedo in a dark and almost-navy shade of midnight. He exuded an air of confidence that only a prince could manage.

"Oh my. You're stunning! Absolutely striking!" His voice caught in his throat as he openly studied me.

"Do you like it? I figured the gold went with the whole sunflower thing." I searched his eyes, watching the play of emotions on his face.

His dimpled smile was devilishly handsome, drawing me close like a magnet.

"You're not a princess tonight. You're a goddess."

He pulled me into him, our flesh meeting in a warm clasp. My pulse quickened, echoing against the empty chamber of his chest.

"There's no denying that chemistry." Gertie walked toward us with a wide grin.

"You're quite the beauty, Gertie. I don't know which of you will be garnering more attention tonight!" Vail bowed, taking Godmother's hand and kissing her knuckles.

"Oh! Hush!" She swatted him away. Her cheeks flushed. "Thank you for inviting me along, Vail. I wouldn't have missed this for the world."

"Ah, yes. Theo's ultimate payback!" Vail said.

"Well, that too. But I'm talking about my goddaughter's time to shine. She deserves this, and you did such a lovely job, bringing it to life for her. I owe you. Thank you." She dipped her head, pressing her lips into a thin line.

"She brought life to me. She's worth every enchanted petal, every crystal's sparkle, and every golden ray of light. No need to thank me. It's me who should be thanking you for raising such a woman."

"You two talk like I'm not here," I spoke up, bottling my embarrassment for another time. I intertwined my fingers with Vail's, tugging him to the back room. "Let's go over the routine once more, please?"

"Of course," he replied. "Can I get you a glass of champagne first, madam?" He turned toward Gertie.

"That would be delightful!" Her eyes shone at his offer.

Vail motioned for a gnome and put in an order for champagne and pastries. The gnome bounced away, flopping his pointed hat from side to side.

"Make yourself at home, Gertie. I expect guests to arrive soon. You'll know some of them. Priscilla specifically asked if you were joining." Vail pulled a chair out at the table next to us.

"Really? Huh. I wonder what she wants." She removed her wand from her pocket and set it on the table before settling into the chair.

"Likely business," Vail called over his shoulder as we made our way to the back.

I opened the door to an old storage room and shoved Vail inside. I ran my fingers through his thick hair and pushed the back of his head down to me. My lips ached for his.

"This isn't practicing," he said between breaths.

"I lied. This is all I needed," I moaned, slipping my tongue into his mouth and stoking the growing fire between us.

He pressed into me, pushing my back against the wall. His erection rubbed across my clit. I hiked my skirt up and swung a leg around him, hooking it at the tip of his hip. His fangs lowered, piercing the underside of my tongue.

"Oh!" I said, pulling back.

"I'm so sorry! I didn't mean for that to happen. Are you all right? Let me take a look." He cupped my chin in his palms and tilted my head up toward the light.

"Vail?" came a voice outside the door. "I can hear you in there."

You've got to be kidding me, I mouthed. I smoothed my skirt down and sighed.

"Let's continue this at the after-party." He shot me a grin, sending a shock wave between my thighs.

He swung open the door to Leo and Ian waiting on the other side.

"We have guests already! All hands on deck. Don't forget, tonight is about money. I don't care who you schmooze, but make sure we're bringing in money by the end of the night, or this place will shut down." Leo's voice was firm and final.

Vail nodded with a taut jerk of his head.

"I'll meet you at the chandelier at showtime. Meanwhile, enjoy your ball, Princess!" He kissed the top of my head and flew out the door with his brothers.

I stepped out to follow him, but Priscilla blocked my path.

"Hello again," she said through those perfect, pouty lips.

Her black eyes rested on cheekbones perched high atop her chiseled face. The way her skin shone in a dewy glow told me she'd fed recently. I wondered if it was one of the poor twins Drake had mentioned the other night.

"Hi," I answered.

"Don't sound so glum, dear. You have nothing to be upset about. On the contrary, I'm here on official business. Scoot back in the room and hear me out." She shooed me into the storage room and shut us both inside.

"Business?" I twisted my hands together behind my back. I had enough to focus on this evening besides making a deal with the devil.

"Mmhmm." Her voice rose in a sickeningly sweet tone. "That little stunt you pulled at The Cave, have you done that again?"

"No."

"Thought not. I can tell by looking at you. Your skin is dull, and you look like you're wasting away. The right magic recharges you." She pushed her shoulders down and looked toward the ceiling, letting out an, "Ahh …"

"I don't understand what happened to me the other night, so …"

"That's why I'm here. What you did back there is beyond anything I've ever seen a princess do. If I was to guess, I'm thinking someone cursed you. And whoever cursed you did a really shitty job. It backfired, and now, instead of losing your magic, it's turned. I can help you find this person and destroy them, you know." She huffed on her nails and polished them across her fur scarf.

"Cursed? I have no enemies. Well, I didn't before I left Poppycock anyway."

"Ah, but you do. You'll figure it out. Anyway, that's your business. My business is, I can use you. But first, I need to train you in the darkness you wield."

"Use me how exactly?" I squinted. My heart began to pound in my chest, and I wondered if Vail could feel it from wherever he'd disappeared off to.

"Bruno—you know, The Bogeyman—and I need a huntress."

"A huntress?" I gasped. "I don't hunt! I love animals!"

"You won't be hunting animals. Well, not the ones you're thinking of. We'll chat more about it later. I only wanted to put the idea in your head. There's a lot of money involved for you and your godmother. You can move out of your leaky cottage and onto a better life if you work with us. But you'll need extensive training, and I'm brutal on my students. It's not for the weak." Her black eyes widened. I could see my reflection staring back.

"I'm not weak."

"Oh, that I know. But you don't know how strong you are either. You're getting there though. Good luck tonight. I can't wait to see the look on your ex's face once he notices you. I hope you have some tricks up your sleeve, and if not, I'll be nearby, watching. Just give me a wink."

"Thanks, but I can handle him myself." I clenched my jaw. The air in the storage room had become stifling.

She pressed her lips together and stared at me for a long minute.

"You could do much more than that. So … much … more …" She flashed an evil grin, tossed her silvery hair behind her shoulders, and left.

I backed into the wall, bracing myself against the sudden fluttering in my brain. I grasped at a nearby sheet, pulling it off an old mirror as I stumbled into the corner.

No. Please no. Not right now.

I took a deep breath and concentrated on keeping my feet on the ground. Then, the feeling passed as fast as it had come. I turned, checking myself in the mirror. It looked to be an almost-exact replica of Mirror Mirror, except it didn't speak.

"Maybe I should swap you out," I said, poking at my reflection.

My bouncy curls hung down the sides of my shoulders, brushing against my ample cleavage. I wore a corset underneath my dress that pushed everything in and up. I couldn't breathe, but by the looks of me tonight, I didn't care. I ran my hand down the glass and squinted.

I didn't recognize the woman staring back at me. She had the same air of confidence I'd seen in Vail. Her chin was tilted up, not down, and her gaze was lethal, stony.

"Look how far you've come," I told myself.

The band began to thumb the strings on their instruments, echoing an energetic tune throughout the halls and drowning out the low murmur of guests filing into the ballroom.

I threw my shoulders back and headed to the attic. Vail planned to introduce me as the special guest first, so we could spend the rest of the evening charming everyone to empty their pockets. I'd smile and wave with my regal stance, and he would dazzle the crowd with his love for me—his fake love for me. He'd made that clear back in the laboratory. I didn't blame him for not having feelings for me. It was too early, and after all, he was a vampire, so I knew it was impossible for him to feel much of anything. But still, I'd let myself fall into his charms … and his bed … and on top of his face. I had no regrets.

I climbed the back staircase and made my way to the chandelier on shaky feet. I strained to pick out the voices I heard down below, but there was no one I recognized. Theo had a loud and obnoxious voice that pompous assholes used when trying to garner attention. There would be no mistaking when he arrived.

"Psst." Vail snuck up behind me.

I jumped, nearly losing my footing.

"Vail Bostwick! You could have given me a heart attack." I put my hand to my chest.

He took my palm from my chest and brought it to his lips. "I'm sorry. Don't be so on edge! There's nothing to worry about," he said.

"Except *him*." I rolled my eyes.

"I looked for him, and he's not made it here yet."

"Oh, I'll know when he's here. Everyone will." I pulled at my heavy earring I'd bought for the wedding I never had.

"Why? Can you smell him? Maybe I can pick up his scent. What's it like?" He stuck his nose in the air and sniffed.

"No. Well, maybe. I've never thought about it." I rubbed my chin and tried to remember if my douche-bag ex smelled like the shit stain he was. "He's just loud."

"Darling! It's been ages! It's so nice to see you. We're running behind because I brought out the special chariot, and these cobblestone roads aren't kind to my golden-hooved horses!" a sharp, nasally voice bellowed below.

"And … he's here," I groaned.

I crouched on the floor, peering down below through a crack.

Theo's thick blond hair had grown out from his usual clipped style. The buttons on his stark white jacket strained against his growing belly, momentarily distracting me from who stood next to him.

"Let me introduce you to my wife, Queen Francine," he said.

Francine paused, sticking her nose in the air before holding her hand out to the guest.

A rush of shock sent me tumbling back and falling on my bottom.

"Who's that?" Vail asked, helping me back to my feet and brushing the dust off of me.

I swallowed the knot in my throat as a thousand different scenarios flooded my thoughts.

"Princess Francine. She's from my patch. We were best friends for a long time, but she became distant when Theo asked me to marry him. I guess I know why now. I bet she's the one who cursed me." The hair on the back of my neck stood on end.

"Cursed?"

A soft flow of music began below, signaling we were about to start.

"Yes, Priscilla has this theory, but anyway, I'll tell you about it later since I can't think." The words flew out of my mouth in one long run-on sentence. I pulled at the collar of my dress and gasped for air.

"Hey! Listen to me! Listen!" Vail grabbed the sides of my head in his massive hands and pressed his forehead to mine. "You never needed this. You don't have to prove yourself, and you know it. This is only an act. It's all it is. It's your closure. Remember the new beginning we discussed? It starts now."

I stared into his eyes. The mere touch of his skin on mine reassured me more than any pep talk could.

"Thank you, Vail. For everything. I hope I can do you proud tonight, too, and bring you lots of money."

"You've brought me so much more than money, Penny."

I gritted my teeth and stared at the ceiling, refusing to let tears well in my eyes. I'd been left at the altar, cast out of Poppycock, and made useless without my magic. But the absolute worst turn of events played out before me tonight. I'd share my very last dance with the vampire who had stolen my heart—in every way.

"Ahem." I cleared my throat, pushing myself from him and climbing atop the chandelier.

I stood, perched on the golden metal rods of the shaky apparatus, and took a deep breath. In a few short moments, I'd find out if my tireless efforts to tell my ex to kiss my ass—in a classy way—would come to fruition or fizzle out.

"Now, remember, I lead, and don't even glance in his direction until after your performance. You don't need any distractions. You should only focus on dazzling the entire room, which shouldn't be hard for you. You look simply stunning."

Vail reached out to me and smoothed my hair back, trailing his knuckles down my shoulder. My flesh prickled at his cool touch.

"Thanks, Vail. But I'm not so sure about this." I curled my fingers along the heavy metal chain, steadying myself. If I could make it down to the floor without falling head over heels on my ass, I would consider tonight a success.

"You have to make an entrance. Trust me on this. The crowd's going to love it, and dumbass Theo will wish he'd never let you go. I know I'd be kicking myself in the ass if I were him and saw you shining like the sun tonight. Especially with the troll he married!" Vail licked his fangs, a habit he'd picked up anytime he mentioned my ex.

I wasn't sure if he was bloodthirsty or turned on.

"You really were Prince Charming in another life, weren't you?"

"I'm an honest vampire. I've nothing to gain from lying to you. You bring a certain warmth to the room … to me. I sensed it the first moment I laid eyes on you in the forest, back when you were such an innocent princess. And look at you now!"

"Ladies, gentlemen, beasts, trolls, creatures of the dark—can I have your attention, please?" Finn said from down below, interrupting Vail.

I craned my neck, peering through the crack again. Finn stood at the center of the ballroom, speaking into a microphone clipped to his vest. I'd never seen him outside of a lab coat, but from what I could tell way up here, the nerdy vamp cleaned up nicely.

The murmur of the crowd quieted.

"Shit. It's time." I swallowed hard, fanning my face, my chest, my armpits. The last thing I needed was a wardrobe malfunction due to the slippery effects of boob sweat.

"You'll be fine," Vail assured me.

"I want to thank you all for being here tonight. It's a very special night for us in so many ways. Bostwick Winery is taking on groundbreaking innovations and ringing in a new era for Morningwood with the help of an extraordinary marketing team.

"I'd like to introduce a special guest we have with us this evening. Her name is Princess Penelope. She came to us in search of a job, but instead, she found a fiancé. Let's welcome the head of marketing and the first woman to join the Bostwick family. Let's give this princess a round of applause and congratulate the happy couple." Finn stepped away, clearing the middle of the floor.

The crowd erupted in cheer. I was probably the first princess to grace their little town.

I bit my lip, stopping it from quivering, and prayed no one asked me about my fake job. I couldn't market a bucket of nuts to a starving squirrel.

"I'll meet you at the bottom," Vail said, tracing his thumb over my mouth and lifting my jaw to meet his gaze. "Chin up, Princess. Tonight, I'm making you my queen. What I do to you in the bedroom, I'm doing to you down there on the dance floor."

The heat from my cheeks drained to between my legs, pooling in warm, electric energy.

He walked to the attic corner and pushed the lever, waving good-bye before scurrying back downstairs to catch me.

The ceiling parted, and the chandelier lurched, lowering to the floor as the orchestra began to play our number. I threw my shoulders behind me and arched my back, twirling down to the center of the room in a flashing display of lights. Even over the sharp notes coming from the orchestra, I heard gasps and awe from the audience. I hung on tighter as I spun faster until the dizzying carousel came to a sudden stop when the music ended in a series of drumrolls.

The crowd went wild, standing up and clapping, hooting and hollering, whistling and cheering.

Vail offered me his hand and plucked me from between the crystals.

"You rode that golden globe down like an empress of the sun." He kissed the back of my knuckles and bowed.

I blushed, noticing for the first time the slight flush in his cheeks too.

The orchestra began to play again, signaling it was showtime.

"Now, start shining." He rose back up, pulling me against the wall of his rigid chest and leading us across the dance floor, our strides fluid and in sync with the soft, classical melody.

His dark eyes never left mine as he swung me through the air in his firm and reassuring grasp. Our bodies swayed together, rocking gracefully across the floor. My heels clicked as he picked up his pace and turned me around to face the crowd. I caught a glimpse of Theo staring at me blankly with his mouth hung wide before Vail spun me back around in his grasp.

"I wanted you to see how stupid he looked." He grinned.

I threw my head back and laughed, cupping Vail's cheek before giving him a quick peck. We strolled about the floor in a whirl of rainbows, smiling at each other as we floated our way to winning the night.

"Are you ready?" I asked as the music began to fade.

He led me to the center of the floor, slowing our steps.

The lights on the chandelier flickered as it rose back up and disappeared into the attic, swinging on its hinges. Flashing neon lights illuminated a confused crowd.

"Always." He gave me a conspiratorial wink.

A faint bassline rang out through the ballroom, vibrating the walls. The velvet curtains hanging from the stage parted, revealing the deejay from The Cave on a turntable, perched high above the orchestra. A dense fog billowed out from under his feet. He gave a faint wave before dropping the bass in a fast-paced beat.

The crowd went wild.

Vail grabbed my waist and struck me across the floor like a match. My slippers sparked, creating a line of fire down our path. He moved beside me as we shook our hips to the rhythm of the music. The crowd cheered with each twerk. He grabbed my hand and twirled me in a blur of heat. I couldn't see what was happening to me, but by the time I was safely back in his arms, my dress had turned into a skintight leather outfit, black as midnight and glowing like a warm ember.

I looked briefly over Vail's shoulder and spotted my godmother. She clicked her tongue and gave me finger guns before stuffing her wand back in her pocket.

"Roll with it." He laughed, picking me up into the air, flipping me, and bringing me back to my feet.

"She's always had my back," I shouted over the music, laughing with him.

He swung a leg over me and slid my body parallel to the floor before twisting me back up into his arms and dipping me in one last grand gesture as the music came to an abrupt stop. My pulse skittered in my chest.

"You didn't look down at your feet once," he said before kissing me, fangs out and on full display.

I grabbed the back of his head and pushed him into me, powerless to resist this unladylike public display of affection.

The guests stood up, clapping and shouting. A ghost let out a wail, witches cackled, and Bruno and the wolves howled. Vail stood us upright, facing the crowd.

"Didn't need to. You'd have caught me if I had fallen." I twitched his nose before we clasped hands and took a bow.

"Get it, girl!" came the deep, gruff voice of an ogre in the back.

The cool flames circling our feet burned out. I had no idea what kind of magic it was, but I had an inkling Priscilla's bitchcraft was involved.

The curtains shut in front of the deejay, and the orchestra slowly began to play again. The energy we'd put into the room was contagious, zapping through the crowd in excited murmurs. I made my way to Godmother, pausing to shake a dozen hands before I could step off the dance floor.

"You make me so proud!" Gertie bounced on her heels, throwing her arms around me.

"Thanks, Godmother. And thanks for the outfit." I chewed my lip, wiggling out of her tight hug.

"Oh. Heavens!" She pulled out her wand and flicked her wrist, magicking my golden dress back on me in a blur of sparkles.

"Thanks." I giggled.

"Sorry. I forgot. You had me mesmerized! I didn't know you knew how to move like that—or you, Vail!" She nudged him with her elbow and raised her brows. "I guess you two really have been practicing all this time."

"Something like that." He smiled. His fangs still hung low in his mouth.

"Well, I'll let you two get on with your shenanigans." She patted my back and yawned. "I'm old. I didn't realize how old until I felt worn out after three glasses of champagne!"

"What? The party's just starting!" I put my hands up, protesting.

"You were the party. I got what I had come for. Besides, I don't want to run into Theo and his bitch of a bride. I never could stand that so-called princess. Hmmph! The look on Theo's face changed from hate to desire to malice while he watched you. If I run into him, I'll magic him into the bunion growing on that ogre's foot over there!" She jerked her head toward a table in the back.

"At least let me take you home," Vail offered.

"Pish-posh! I can enchant the steering wheel and drive myself. Just bring Penelope back home safely, if you don't mind. I won't give you until midnight or whatever those old rules are. Take all night if you want, but be back by dawn." She squeezed my hand and pressed her lips together, searching my eyes for understanding.

"I'll get her there." Vail put his arm over my shoulders, mashing me into his side.

"Thank you." She dipped her head and kissed me good-bye.

"See you soon. And keep Pumpkin out of my room, please! I don't want him in bed with me again tonight," I shouted after her, but she'd already disappeared into the crowd.

Vail placed his hand on my back and guided me away, toward a group of well-dressed gnomes. We worked the room for an hour as I proudly let him put me on display. We both wooed the guests with bullshit tales of our upcoming nuptials and how we'd met. He weaved the lab's cause into conversations and made investing in the cure sound so good that even I considered donating to the winery. But then I remembered I was broke because of the asshole here with us tonight.

I raised my chin and searched the room. My eyes fell on Theo's. He wore a scowl matching his bride's. She twisted the wedding ring on her finger as she looked from me to him and back again.

"Vail?" I tugged at his elbow during a lull in his conversation with an elf.

"Yes, darling?" he asked.

"I think it's time. I want to introduce you to … *Theo*." I took a deep breath and straightened my spine.

Vail's smile faded. "Of course."

I snapped my eyes across the room, casting an icy stare in Theo's direction.

"Let's go." I hooked my arm in Vail's and marched across the dance floor to the other side of the room.

Vail stiffened next to me. Theo shifted his weight from one foot to the other. The knot in his throat bounced as we approached.

I opened my mouth to greet him but was interrupted by a whirl of black hissing past me in a rush of cold air. Before I could blink, Theo's headless body collapsed in a pool of blood. His head rolled across the floor, thumping against my slippers with a sickening thud. He still appeared slack-jawed.

Francine began to shriek.

TWELVE

VAIL

I PUSHED PENELOPE BEHIND me, shielding her from the blur of the black-cloaked figures closing in on us. Screams erupted from the crowd as the guests trampled each other underfoot. Werewolves transformed into their beastly selves, ripping the black-cloaked men apart in a splattering of blood. I roared as I recognized The Council's emblem etched in red across their chests.

Priscilla stood on the stage with dead eyes, outstretching her arms and muttering something under her breath. A heavy fog rolled through the room, boiling the skin on the attackers' ankles, slowing them down.

"Help!" Penelope cried as a Council member burst from the crowd, landing on his feet in front of us.

He hissed, showing us his entire smile had been replaced with fangs. He wiped the blood from his mouth on the back of his arm.

"Tsk, tsk. Someone's been meddling where they shouldn't," he said, crouching and readying to pounce.

I flashed my fangs, holding my arms out to the sides and blocking him from getting to Penelope.

Drake leaped through the air and grabbed the vampire's head, twisting his neck. His spine cracked like a whip, snapping in half. He kicked the vampire's lifeless body and dived back into the chaos as quickly as he'd appeared.

Penelope screamed, taking off in the direction of the door. I grabbed her and pulled her toward a corner, guarding our backs. A wolf let out a mournful howl, followed by more.

"Fuck! That's not good," I shouted, clenching my fists. "I need to get you somewhere safe."

Bruno's dark figure rose above the crowd, bursting forth from his suit and revealing scaly red skin. Clawed limbs shot out from under him. A pair of bat-like wings grew from his back amid a row of thick spikes and a long, tapered tail. His face flattened into a long snout. Smoke escaped from his slitted nostrils.

"Get her out of here!" Leo shouted, rushing toward us.

Bruno roared, shooting a six-foot flame out of his mouth and setting a group of both vampires and guests on fire. The fire coursed through the crowd, lighting the fog in one big smoke pit.

A vampire appeared from the smog and pulled a stake from under his cloak. Before I could react, he drove the stake into Leo's back. Leo's eyebrows scrunched together as he fell to the ground.

"What're you going to do now that your dear leader's gone?" The vampire opened his bloody mouth and laughed.

"First, I'm going to kill you. Then, I'm going to kill your friends. When you're gone, I'm going to finish what we started."

I rushed full speed to the vampire, entangling my body with his on the floor. My knuckles crushed into his jaw, sending bits of blood and fang flying from his mouth. I rolled myself on top of him, digging my knees into his rib cage. He strained against me, grabbing hold of my arm and wrestling the stake from my hand.

Ian ran at us, stomping his foot into the vampire's nose. The crunch of bone rang out over another vampire's dying screams coming from Bruno's mouth. I wrapped my fist around the stake and drove it into my enemy's chest, twisting it deeper and deeper until his body began to ash.

"Come on!" Ian shouted, helping me to my feet.

I rushed back toward Leo and my brothers, who stood, circling our fallen leader.

"I'm so sorry." My knees buckled as I fell down next to him.

"It's all right," Leo croaked. "I'm dying on a battlefield amid my brothers. I couldn't have asked for a more honorable way to go." He brought his hand to his face and gave a limp salute, groaning with each movement. "Now, save the girl and save the brotherhood. For the cause," he said before his lips turned to ash and blew away.

Drake roared and ran back into the fight. I stood up, readying myself to join him.

Finn tugged my arm, jerking me back. "Don't do it. Don't you dare. You take her back home and stay there. Let us handle this. You know as much as I do, we need her. It was his dying words. Save her."

I drew my attention back to Penelope, who sat, huddled in the corner, rocking back and forth on her knees. She was whispering something under her breath, sending sparks of fire out from underneath her. As much as I wanted to avenge the night and wipe out every last piece of filth in the ballroom, I wanted to save the princess more.

"Penelope! We have to go!" I shouted, pulling her up and slinging her over my shoulder.

We rushed out the back door and into the vineyard before I set her down and allowed her to catch her breath.

"Who are they?" she gasped, stumbling toward a grapevine. She held her hand out, bracing herself and heaving.

"The Council. They know what we've been working on. I'm just not sure they know who you are—or what you can do. Otherwise, if they did, you'd likely be dead by now," I growled, pacing back and forth among the rows of grapes before returning to her side.

Guests' cars sped down our gravel drive, kicking up clouds of dust.

"So, they don't know?" she asked through ragged breaths.

A sprinkling of ash floated down on us, catching in her hair.

"What now?" I said, plucking a flake of ash from her hair. I turned my face to the direction the ash had blown in from. A blaze of smoke rose from the woods, where Penelope's cottage stood.

She followed my gaze. "Godmother?" Her voice caught in her throat as she realized where the fire was coming from. "No. This isn't happening. No." She violently shook her head. "They don't know! You said they didn't know!" She pressed her palms flat against my chest and pushed me away.

"I said I wasn't sure." I held out my hands, stopping her.

She whirled on her heels, running headfirst into the woods.

A knot grew in the pit of my stomach like a heavy stone, weighing me down.

"It's not safe!" I shouted, running after her.

"I don't fucking care! That's my family in there!" she shouted back, leaping over a fallen trunk.

I caught up to her, scooping her in my arms and running us toward her house in a flash.

The heat from the fire lingered throughout the trees, trapped in the dense wood.

Penelope pulled up her dress, covering her nose and coughing as we neared the flaming cottage. The fire roared, crumbling what was left of her home.

"Godmother!" she shouted, wiggling out of my grasp.

I grabbed her and pulled her back. "Stop!" I said, my voice edged with command. "You're staying here. I'll go!"

I ran my hands through my hair and made my way toward the door. Pumpkin lay, smashed across the front stoop, his seeds spilling out over the dirt. I glanced over my shoulder. Trevor and Grump circled Penelope's feet. Otto swooped out from the house, clutching a coughing Mirror Mirror in his grasp and whining. The mirror shook his head at me.

The front of the house collapsed, sending a rush of flames and ash into my face.

"Ah!" I screamed, clutching my eyes and stumbling backward.

"Vail!" Penelope rushed to me, pulling me away. "Don't do it!" she sobbed. "Don't. It's too late. You can't save her." She pointed her finger in the air.

I squinted, rubbing the soot from my eyes. A whirlwind of powder-blue smoke sparkled up and away into the night sky, disappearing among the stars.

I'd never seen the death of a fairy godmother. They were sometimes as old as vampires. But I knew when they left earth, they returned to the stars from whence they had come, turning into a twinkle and eventually a wish.

Penelope fell to her knees and wailed, rocking back and forth. She placed her palms in the dirt and buckled, coughing in deep, gut-wrenching heaves. I put my arm around her waist and dragged her from the smoke. Her skin grew slick with sweat.

"No! Leave me!" she screamed, kicking her feet and fighting against me. "I don't want to go. Let me be! I didn't get to say good-bye! I didn't get to grow the patch she wanted! I didn't practice my spells, Vail! I could have saved her! I should have been here!" she wailed, convulsing with each sob.

I winced, carrying her away from the cottage. The remaining frame collapsed, crumbling into one big bonfire of blue smoke. She wiggled against me, her face twisted in pain. She was barely recognizable as the woman who had flown across the dance floor in a beam of sunlight only hours earlier.

I pressed her trembling body against mine as I took her to the clearing and set us down on a damp layer of moss. I cradled her in my arms and let her cry, but no matter how tight I held her, I couldn't keep her from leaving. She vanished from my grasp without a pop of glitter or confetti. She simply faded away and out of my arms. I knew by the misery in her face, she wasn't coming back.

Her army of misfits howled beside me.

I clutched my empty chest and cried out. The familiar edge of heartbreak sliced through me, haunting my memory with the awful emotion I'd long forgotten.

I needed to find Penelope. I had to save her, save the cause, and save myself.

AN UPDATE FROM THE DESK OF FRITZI COX

DEAR READER,

When I wrote my previous note at the beginning of this story, I had no idea as to Penelope's whereabouts. The minimal information she'd offered during our rare meetings was hardly anything I could use in my research to travel back to her supernatural dimension. I scoured Morningwood for more clues on her disappearance or the vampire laboratories she'd mentioned. But after weeks with little development, I decided to return home and invent her ending myself, giving her the happily ever after she deserved.

It wasn't long after I settled back into my daily routine at home that I received a phone call from the Outer Forks City Jail. A hysterical Penelope had somehow found me. In between gut-wrenching sobs, she confessed what had happened to her dear godmother and that douche bag Theo. But for security's sake, I stopped her before she said too much. Instead, I told her that I was on my way to bail her out of whatever trouble she'd managed to get herself into.

Thus, my story isn't over, and neither is hers.

In this book, I wrote what I'd learned from our brief conversations to the best of my knowledge. Names were changed, and details were embellished, but the mischief in Morningwood remains, and as a dutiful reporter, I am eager to investigate it.

Continue reading Penelope's adventures in *Royally Cursed*, book two in the VILF series.

ACKNOWLEDGMENTS

As always, thank you to my daughter, my princess. There's not a perfect flower that could have bloomed you. May you always blaze your own path and find your own magic. I love you so much.

Thank you to my amazing editor, Jovana; my awesome cover designer, Lori; my talented graphic designer, Katherine; and my badass assistant, Kim. DTF! I'm so lucky to have such special sisters in my Princess Patch.

Thank you to my fellow writers who hold my hand, the bookstagrammers and readers who keep me going, and the wine industry for motivation.

Thank you to my friend J, who has the cleverest brain I've ever come across. Brainstorming with you is always a party. Your support will forever be life-changing.

Thank you to The D for supporting me in every step of my new life even if I'm summoning farty wind spirits instead of butterflies. You're the real Prince Charming.

ABOUT THE AUTHOR

FRITZI COX IS A dark soul with a wicked sense of humor. She regularly bathes in the blood of her enemies while sipping champagne and hashtagging her vibes. She's fond of plotting mayhem, writing spellbinding twists, and tickling her readers with an over-the-top sense of humor. Rumor has it, her alter ego, Kat Addams, is her spirit animal. Or is it the other way around? Either way, expect Fritzi to keep you on your toes!

You can find Fritzi in her DTF Reader Group or follow her at the links below. Be sure to subscribe to Fritzi's newsletter to keep up-to-date with new releases, sneak peeks, exclusive content, and more!

AUTHOR'S NOTE

Some of the links will lead you to Fritzi's main pen name, Kat Addams. If you're looking for contemporary romcom without the dark, spooky magic, then please check out Kat's books. Kat and Fritzi share a newsletter, a Facebook page, and Instagram. They're a two-for-one special.

Newsletter + FREE book!
https://kataddams.com/free-book

Fritzi's Website: www.fritzicox.com

Kat's Website: www.kataddams.com

DTF Reader Group:
www.facebook.com/groups/
DirtyToughFemales

Facebook:
www.facebook.com/KatAddamsAuthor

Instagram:
www.instagram.com/authorkataddams/

Bookbub:
www.bookbub.com/authors/fritzi-cox

Goodreads:
www.goodreads.com/author/show/
20723385.Fritzi_Cox

OTHER BOOKS BY KAT ADDAMS

DIRTY SOUTH SERIES

Hotty Toddy (Free for newsletter subscribers:
https://kataddams.com/free-book)
Grit and Grind
Nashvegas Nights
Mr. Big Ego
Mayday

DTF (DIRTY. TOUGH. FEMALE.) SERIES

On the Rox
Cream-Pied
Whip It Out
Just the Tip

FU (FORKS UNIVERSITY FASHION ACADEMY) SERIES

Sew Basic
Sew Haute

BUCK OFF RANCH SERIES

Josie Thatcher, Cowboy Catcher

PARANORMAL ROMANTIC COMEDY, WRITING AS FRITZI COX

VILF SERIES

Ghosted
Royally Drained
Royally Cursed

For a complete listing of Kat Addams's books, visit https://kataddams.com